Ghost of a Chance

A PARANORMAL THRILLER

Ray Wenck

Glory Days Press

Editor: Jodi McDermitt

Cover: Molly Wenck

Published By: Glory Days Press

ISBN: 978-0996830812

Dedication

This work is dedicated to my daughter, April, who has worked hard to make my works more noticeable and me more presentable to the public eye. Thank you and I love you.

Acknowledgement

With any novel there are many people who help to make the creation possible. That is especially true for this, my first self-published work. I had no clue how to go about self-pubbing. If not for the assistance of my friend and fellow author Constance Phillips, this story might never have been told.

I would like to thank Tanja, my writing buddy, for her support and encouragement. My editor Jodi McDermitt and graphic designer Molly Wenck also deserve my thanks.

I would also like to thank Steve and Nancy Butcher and their wonderful staff at the Nutcracker Family Restaurant for allowing me to sit there and write on numerous occasions.

Lastly, a special thanks to my family and growing list of friends for their continued support and encouragement. Even with all the voices in my head, some days yours are the only ones I hear to keep me going.

CHAPTER

One

If they thought by killing me it was the end of the matter, they didn't know me very well. If I never gave up when I was alive, no way would I quit now, just because – well ... Of course, the restrictions death puts on you tends to make revenge a little more difficult. But I had to try – something. Too many lives depended on me, including that of my wife, whom I had never met.

I died days before we would meet. At first I didn't understand I was dead. I do now. It's the only possible explanation. How my demise occurred is still a mystery, though. If only I hadn't gotten involved. But then, that wouldn't have been me. Besides, my future wife and I might've died anyway. At least now there's still a chance I can save her, even though she'll never know who I am.

I had many questions, but acceptance of my new situation is not something worth dwelling on at the moment. There's still too much to do and so much to learn. Knowing that there could have been someone in my life has only served to increase my determination to find a way back. I had wasted too much time already.

Upon arrival at wherever this was, I'd taken a quick look around, but my mind whirled in confusion and desperation. Now, spinning slower this time, I took in my surroundings with a more trained eye. Nothing. Just endless, translucent, almost cloud-like flooring. Where the hell was I? One moment I was standing in an alley facing three men—the next, what? I closed my eyes to bring the scene back to mind.

The putrid smell of the restaurant dumpster to my left rose to memory's call. My three would-be assailants were stretched out in front of me. One was down and hurt; one down and stunned. I remembered the twitch of a smile tug at my lips as I watched the unhurt third man try to decide what to do. Another ten seconds and the confrontation would be over.

The punk to the left struggled to rise and the last man standing bent to help him. It was time to end this but before I could step forward, my opponent froze. There it was, the thing I missed. No, not missed; reacted too slowly to. The quick glance past me. Then came the breeze, but that wasn't right either. It was a chill that ran up my spine, springing the hairs on the back of my neck to life. And even as I began to make a move, something inside told me I was already too late.

I flung my hands to the back of my head as if swatting at bees, but found no bloody hole. Patting my body as if it were on fire, I failed to find any signs of a life-ending wound. But in those seconds, any doubt of my situation fled giving way to my new reality.

I was dead.

Unsure how long I stood there glazed over after the acceptance, I shook my head, raised my hands and screamed, "No! Not yet! I refuse to accept this. Do you hear me? I deny my death."

With fire blazing in my eyes, I began walking. There had to be someone or something to tell me where I was. Information was the key and the faster I accumulated that knowledge, the better the chance I would have to get back to earth and save some lives. I would not allow failure when so many people could die. It wasn't fair. I may not have always done right, but I had always believed in righteousness.

White tendrils drifted in front of me like shredded cloth and separated before my eyes. "Is anyone out here?" But my words went unanswered and carried out into the endless space. Maybe this was my hell: to wander in endless solitaire. Well, that may be, and that was all right, but I had something to do first. I stopped and did another slow pivot. The wisps died down, and the distance was once more clear and just as barren.

My frustration rose, reaching the exploding point. There had to be another way. Time was running out, but for whom? I had to act now, but who was I saving? I understood so little of the potential threat, only that it existed and could cause massive death and injuries. What made matters worse was that I was the only one who knew of the danger.

However, between the distraction of dying and exploring my new landscape, I had wasted valuable time. I wasn't even sure if days passed here as they did on Earth. Had it been seconds or centuries since I … ? The anxiety caused a vibration through what passed for my physical being, edging me closer toward panic.

I had to learn my way around this place and quick. First, I had to discover where I was. Was this heaven or hell? If I was dead, where was the white light that guided me home? Had I missed it? I'd like to say there was beauty. I wish I could tell you at long last I'd found peace. But in truth, I couldn't settle my spirit down long enough to relax or enjoy my new home. Nervous energy pulsed through me; a creation of the resentment I felt leaving earth, knowing what I knew.

Looking around was no help. How could I figure out where I was if I couldn't see anything? Damn it, there should at least be signs. If this was heaven, I was lied to big time. If it was hell, it made sense. For one, I would go crazy looking at nothing for eternity. And two, let's face it; I was no boy scout while alive, even though I only tried to help people who couldn't help themselves. Just because most of my methods were illegal shouldn't have been enough to judge me and send me to this—this endless fog.

But even in fighting through the confusion, I was determined to find my way back. The lives of a lot of innocent people depended on me, I think. The longer I was here, the more confused I became. No! I pushed out with my mind in an effort to clear away the cobwebs of doubt. I knew what I knew, and it was real. My death was a result of that knowledge: proof of the threat's validity.

With renewed determination, I began to peer deeper into the haze and quickly became lost in wide-eyed amazement. It took every bit of will to pull myself away from my discoveries and remember the impending death of thousands. Still, I might have given up on going back, as overwhelmed as I was by what I'd been watching—the various threads of my future life; a life that would forever go unfulfilled--when I heard The Voice.

CHAPTER

Two

"Hello, Chance."

If I still could have shit, I would have. He scared ten years off my life, but did that matter anymore. I turned to see a tall, radiant-looking black man looking at me. His short hair was speckled with gray. He stood in a casual stance, hands clasped behind his back. His mouth was unsmiling, but his eyes danced with delight. He had enjoyed startling me. Unable to form words, I envisioned more than felt my heart caught in my throat.

"I see you've discovered the threads."

"The threads?" I said, confused.

Now he did smile as he approached me.

"Man, am I glad to see you. Actually, I'm happy to see anyone. Can you help me?"

"Of course. That *is* why I'm here."

My mouth worked up and down, trying to focus on what to ask next. I went with the query fueled by anger. "You're here to help me? What the hell took you so long? I've been looking for help since I got," I stretched my arms, "here."

He smiled, quick and humorless. His jeans were well worn and his red-flannel shirt hung open over a blue t-shirt. He moved effortlessly, like he was gliding.

"You'll forgive me. You're not my only charge. Usually new arrivals are too wound up to need me right away."

"Well, maybe they're wound up *because* they need you right away. I've got some major problems and need some answers."

That humorless smile again. "Yes, I'm sure you do. I'm sure I know what the first ones will be, too."

I paused as if I were being played.

"Why don't we go slow and let me explain. My name is Les. I'm your transition counselor."

"Transition counselor? You mean like in high school?"

"In a way. I will do my best to answer your questions and get you acclimated. Then it will be up to you to adjust – or not."

I didn't like the tone of this and started to pace like some caged animal. Les made it sound like we were filling out an application for a new apartment. I didn't want a new lease, at least not just yet. I wanted to rent space in a human body for a short time.

Facing him, I started to speak, but he held up his hand and shook his head. "Let me just stop you now. To answer your first question, there is no way to go back."

That did stop me. "What? You can read my mind?'

"Everyone asks that question."

"But-but this is really important."

He put his hands behind his back and shook his head. "I don't think you're ready for me yet." He turned and walked away.

He stood in the background with his hands still clasped behind him, watching me as I bounced around my new reality like some cosmic pinball. He eyeballed me with focused intent, as though he had paid an admission to my one-man show. When his steady gaze became too much, I turned on him.

"What are you looking at?" I demanded. My hands clenched and opened.

"I was just waiting for you to settle down, Chance."

Chance? No one called me Chance. With a last name like Swift, everyone called me Tom or Swifty.

"How do you know my name?"

"Seriously?"

All right, I'll admit; it was a dumb question. I moved on to the next obvious one.

"Where am I?"

"That's still for you to decide."

Then it was my turn. "Seriously?"

He continued to stare. Whatever was left of my patience was quickly turning to annoyance.

"Who are you and why are you here?"

"Ah. Now we're getting somewhere. As I told you, my name is Les, and as I said I am your transition counselor."

"Transition counselor, huh? Well, how about transitioning me back to earth?"

Les sighed and shook his head.

"Look, it's just for a few hours," I pleaded.

Les cocked his head to the side like a dog trying to understand his owner's words. I made another attempt.

"You don't understand. A lot of lives are at stake. I'm not asking for myself." When I got no reaction from Les I slapped my hands on either side of my face.

What was I to do?

I was desperate now and I lost it a little.

"Listen, you heartless bastard. Have you been dead for so long you've forgotten how to feel? I'm talking about thousands of lives lost for no reason, lives that can be saved if you just give me the chance to go back. I promise I'll come right back."

"I'm sorry, but that's impossible. And there is only One who can save lives."

Anger exploded inside my head. A red haze descended over my eyes.

"How can you be so cold? These are human beings we're talking about, not some long dead ghosts. Or do you want them all to die? Is that it? Do you have some sort of spirit world quota to meet? Answer me, damn you!"

I advanced on Les, my clenched hands forming the fists that had helped so many people with their strength and brutality ready for battle once more. I wanted to grab Les and shake understanding into him, but as I closed to within swinging distance, a strange twinkle lit his eyes and the corners of his mouth turned up in a sarcastic smile.

I realized I couldn't touch him, but it didn't stop me from trying. "You have to send me back!" I screamed and grabbed for his shoulders. My hands didn't so much pass through him as much as he just wasn't there when I reached. He didn't physically step away. His body sort of bent backward out of reach then reformed in front of me.

His smile broadened. Again he said, "Seriously?"

I turned, squeezing my head between my hands. My brain was full of such an intense rage I thought I might die, which would have been interesting since I was already dead.

I walked away from Les. Frustration and helplessness were unfamiliar emotions to me. The stress was more than I could handle. Something strange crept down my face. Swiping the moisture away, I stared at my wet fingertips in shocked disbelief.

Tears?

I stood there, head bowed, and let the tears roll. I couldn't remember the last time I cried. Then, clearer than any image my mind should be able to create, I was there. There in the last moment I had cried. It was the day before our deployment was over. My unit was being shipped home. We had made it. We would survive and go home.

But the joy was premature. Our platoon was attacked on our way back to base. When reinforcements arrived, only three of us were still alive. I cried then, as my friend Private Michael Newman died next to me. I hadn't thought about that for a long time, and especially not so vividly. With time the images had become grainier until I was able to wall up my mates' deaths in my repression vault.

The tear tracks dried in long streaks on my face. My awareness of them surprised me as if somehow I had heightened senses. I wiped them away and looked at my damp hands. Wow! Who'd have thought being dead could be so emotional?

Les placed a hand on my shoulder. I looked at it, wondering how he could touch me since I couldn't make physical contact with him.

"I'm sorry, Chance. It will take time for you to accept and process your demise. That's why I'm here, to help you through the tough times. I will answer all your questions and hopefully guide you toward your ultimate eternity."

Sighing, I glanced over my shoulder at Les. His face was calm and expressionless, except for his eyes. I recognized the emotion reflected there—pity. My anger faded. My once beating heart came crashing down. *Should you be able to feel such pain when you're dead?*

For the first time I took a serious look around. The foggy surroundings made it appear that I was standing inside a cloud. Though I had the feeling there was vast space all around me, I couldn't see anything past my own cloud. There was nothing but Les and me. If this was heaven, I was going to get bored real fast. I didn't know if I was an angel or a ghost, but I was pretty sure I wasn't a demon. I think I'd be a lot less comfortable. But maybe hell was a state of mind and not a place. Staring at nothing for eternity would certainly be hell to me.

"So where is this place, anyway?"

Les' hand fell from my shoulder and he smiled.

"Let's just say it's like a holding area."

"A holding area? What, like purgatory? I thought the church or God did away with that."

"In a way, yes, but it is more of a place for you to adjust to your situation before you find permanence elsewhere."

"So I could still be headed for hell, huh?"

"That remains a possibility."

"Then what am I? If I'm not an angel or a demon, am I a ghost?"

"You are simply yourself, or if you prefer, your soul."

"What does that make you, my soul mate?"

CHAPTER

Three

On earth I may not have always done good things, but whatever I did, my actions were meant with good intentions and a kind heart. Of course, there are many people still walking around down there—and a few who aren't—who might argue that statement.

Sometimes the way I handled a particular situation was not always legal. However, it was always done in the pursuit of justice—if not in the eyes of the law, then at least in the minds of the victims I helped and their families. But I couldn't shake the concern that time was running out for a lot of people. Regardless of my current situation, there had to be a way for me to help them. What I needed was more information.

My mind whirled as I studied my surroundings and searched for possible solutions. I just didn't know enough. Depression began to settle over me.

Les read my mind. "I'm sorry, but there's just no way of going back. Almost everyone I have ever dealt with has wanted to go back. Some never accept their situation. Your best recourse is acceptance. The sooner you adjust to your death, the sooner you can enjoy your potential rewards."

"Huh! And what potential rewards does hell offer? Tropical climate?" He made no reply. "Your job is to get me to move on. But what if I can't let go?"

Les frowned. "Eventually you will. Sometimes souls reside here for a very long time. It's difficult to accept.

Believe me, I know. But in the end it's for the best. I'm sure there are others here who are waiting for you. You should reunite with them. It will ease the pain you feel now."

My thoughts collided against each other, keeping me confused. With so much to think about, I was unable to focus on the one thing that mattered most. There had to be a way to go back to earth or to at least send a warning.

I began to pace again. The space was just too large. When I looked up, a wall of white had materialized twenty feet in front of me. I walked toward the cloud-like barrier, but nearing it, the wall retracted as if anticipating that I would want to go further. Changing direction, I strode toward the opposite wall. The same thing happened, but when I looked back at the first wall it had resumed its original position. Weird.

"So, does my cubicle adjust its dimensions to meet my needs?

"Since the original size was only a starting point, the dimensions are only restricted by your own imagination. If you feel you need more space, simply create it."

"Why is my holding cell so plain?" I asked.

"Because you haven't made it yours yet."

Huh?

"Les, how long have you been doing this transportation guide thing? Please tell me I'm not your first."

Les studied me my actions with a strange look on his otherwise smug face.

"Am I being too vague?"

"Well, I don't know. Did you walk to school or carry a lunch?"

Les broke into a sincere smile. He had a good smile when he did it for real.

"Perhaps you're not asking the right questions or you're incapable of understanding the answers. And for the record, it's transition counselor, and no, you are not my first."

"Okay. Don't get your—whatever you wear, if anything, in a bunch. But seriously, what gives with the décor?"

"You haven't even attempted to explore your new world yet, so it remains as it was when you arrived. Think of it as an apartment you have just moved into. You have to add your own personal touches and decorate it the way you want."

"Oh. So if I want a picture hanging from that cloud over there, I just put it up?"

"Exactly."

"Is there like a Kohls or a Sears here? Where do I get the home furnishings?"

Les again studied me. I recognized that look. He thought I was a bit dense. "From your memories, Chance. You envision what you want and if you can form that picture, it will appear."

A thought came to me. I pictured my apartment. I looked around. My disappointment must have shown on my face.

Les frowned. "Chance, you cannot visualize yourself back to life. It's not going to happen. No matter how bad you wish it, you cannot be alive again. I'm sorry. Now try again. You can do this. Concentrate."

I realized he was trying to help me by getting me to focus on anything else and keep my mind off being dead. Deciding to humor him for a while until I could pump him for more info, I thought about something for a moment and then looked at my vaporous walls. "Huh; it didn't work."

"Try doing it with real purpose. You have to visualize what you want, not just have the idea." He turned and said, "Here, watch."

Les extended his hand with a sweeping motion and a beautiful landscape covered the west wall. Mountains filled the distance. A calm lake with bright blue water reflected the mountains that towered above and just beyond. Pine tree forests surrounded the lake on two sides.

My mouth hung open. The scene was so real. I felt like I was there. I wanted to hike to those mountains and climb up to the highest point. Closing my eyes for a moment, I felt a light breeze ruffle my hair. The scent of pine filled my nostrils. I felt warm all over.

Was the visage real or a creation of some distant memory?

I looked at Les in awe and waited for an explanation.

He shrugged. "Rocky Mountain National Park. One of my favorite places in the world."

"That's amazing. You've obviously been there. The detail is so real. You must know it very well."

A sudden, sorrowful look passed through Les' eyes. "Yes, I knew it very well."

A long silence stretched out between us. Les was somewhere else in his thoughts, so I let him be. *Did the scene have something to do with his death?* He blinked hard a few times and was back in the present. A few moments later, the scene faded away.

He cleared his throat. "Try it. It's not that hard."

I thought for a few seconds about what I wanted. I'd been to plenty of beautiful areas, or at least they would have been beautiful if they hadn't have been in war zones, but I tossed those images aside. Then it came to me.

I closed my eyes and nodded my head like I was Jeannie from the TV show. When I opened them again a picture of my platoon mates magically floated in midair. We were all smiles then, having just received word of our withdrawal. We were going home. What we didn't know was it would be the last time we would all be happy and alive.

The memory transported me back to the outskirts of a small village with barely more than a half dozen mud huts with thatched roofs. We were a bunch of well-trained young men and had survived many a firefight. Perhaps we'd grown complacent, knowing our time was short. Or maybe our own feelings of invulnerability had let our guards down. Whatever the reason, we walked into the ambush like a group of raw recruits.

The first shots took out the LT and our sergeant, leaving us leaderless. I took over command and coordinated a successful counterattack without losing another life. We held that village for two days, fighting off one attack after another before being relieved.

We returned to camp exalted; the adrenaline buzz of battle still racing hard through our veins. The bonds of friendship formed over the long months we were there had solidified into iron. Time after time we'd repelled each assault, saving each other's lives on numerous occasions. It was a crime to have survived everything we had been through, only to lose it all a day before being shipped out. Death was as unfair as life had been.

I never really recovered from that loss of brotherhood. I saw that now but the revelation came too late to matter.

I started to speak but choked on the words. Clearing my throat, I tried again. "Would you happen to know if any of the guys are here?"

Les shook his head. "These aren't my memories and I try not to intrude. Unless you let me in, you are the only one who can explore your memories." He put his hand on my shoulder again. "My friend, you have so much to learn. If you will allow me to, I will guide you through this process and you can go on from there. Once you have understanding you will find that anything is possible here."

A light went on inside my head. *Anything?* That sounded like a possibility to me. Regardless of what Les said, I was determined to find a way to warn those people about the fate that awaited them. Yes, I needed information, so I would explore my new world. After all, in Les' own words, anything was possible.

CHAPTER

Four

I got lost in the endless possibilities of my now nonexistent future, especially when I found the thread that led to the woman who would be my wife.

Les showed me how to travel the threads. The threads were the various alternative paths my life might have taken based upon the decisions I made at the time. Each choice created an alternate lifeline, or as Les would say, "the paths not chosen."

The rules were simple. You could follow any thread backwards to it's origination point but you could not follow your reality thread back past the point of your death. To find the secondary routes, one had to first find the reality thread. This one was thicker than the others. The reality thread continued forward as the most likely life path had you not died. From there you had but to jump in any direction to enter an alternate reality and follow it back to where you made the decision that caused the branch or forward to see where it led. The exploration was so fascinating a new arrival could get lost for an eternity, as apparently, I had.

The part about not being able to go past your death held my interest. I speculated that was because someone could try to go back in time and attempt to change a certain outcome that perhaps would allow them to live longer. I let the idea percolate as Les talked.

Rules were created because at some point someone had figured out how to do something that others felt was either dangerous or had a long-term negative impact on the population. If going back through your life was banned, then it had to be because the Powers That Be were afraid it might be possible to go back and affect a change that could throw the future into chaos. If the fear existed, then so did the possibility. My guess was someone had already tried and succeeded, or at least came close. My theory could have been way off, but the possibility gave me hope so I went with it.

The problem was that once I began following threads of what my life could have been, I lost track of time. It was easy to be mesmerized by what I was seeing. I couldn't stop riding the threads.

In one alternate life I was in prison. Three small threads extended from there; I died in prison, I escaped, and I was paroled. Another variation had me getting gunned down by the police, while a lesser version had the shooters being members of a drug cartel.

There seemed to be a concerning high percentage of threads that had me dying by violent means. A few had me living long happy lives, at least to the point I'd stopped riding those particular strands. However, the best thread was also the second thickest one, making it one of the most likely of possibilities; the one where I met my wife.

Surprised, I was unable to tear my eyes away from her. She looked so real and so...right. I popped out of the thread feeling warm. The warmth faded to sadness.

"Why are some of the threads more real looking?" I asked Les. "I mean, with some it's like I'm actually there."

"The more vivid the scene, the more likely was the reality. The choice you had to make at the moment the thread begins gives that thread the highest possibility of occurring based on your past decisions or current situation."

"So, although all of these could have happened, the thicker threads had the best chance of coming true?"

"Exactly."

I pointed. "This one is the thickest thread. This is probably the direction my life would've taken had I not made what turned out to be my final choice."

Les could see the thread, but only I could see what it contained.

"Yes, but I have to warn you. These images may cause you the most pain. You may not want to follow this thread for a while."

I thought about what Les said. Maybe he was trying to protect me, but I was intrigued and had to know. Besides, if this was the most likely outcome, perhaps there was a clue as to how I might get a message through to earth. But even as that thought began fading to the background, I knew I would travel that thread just to be near my wife.

"How could I not be curious as to how my life might have turned out? I wouldn't have wanted to know the future when I was alive, but now that I'm not, what harm could it do?"

Les nodded and gave a sympathetic smile. "I know," he said. "You have to look."

With all thoughts of my desperation to reach Earth pushed aside, I swallowed hard and dove into my best future.

CHAPTER

Five

There I was, strolling through an older part of the city I'd only been to a few times. I felt happy and started singing to myself. It was early on a breezy but warm summer eve. Stomach growling, I searched for someplace to eat.

I must not have been aware of the danger that would destroy so many lives at that point, which meant I never went to that restaurant and overheard the conversation. Something had changed.

This future reality had me entering a diner I spied mid-block on a downward sloping road. I sat in a window booth and scanned the menu. When the waitress came to take my order, I froze. My heart skipped a beat. She was the most beautiful woman I had ever seen. Our eyes locked for just a moment and it was all over for me. She blushed and smiled, probably feeling uneasy about my open mouthed stare. Her name tag read, "Monica."

"Hi," I managed, but needed prompting before I could remember to order. As she walked away my eyes followed her. No, not checking out her ass. I mean really watched her. I had never had that feeling pass through me before. Whatever future me was feeling on alternate earth, I felt as well. Even though this was a virtual reality both my physical and emotional reactions couldn't have been more real.

I wanted to get to know her; had to get to know her. The thought held an urgency that quickened my non-existent pulse. Nothing was more important. To know that even after all I'd been through, not counting dying and all the questionable things I'd done in my life, to find there was something good and pure waiting for me down the line was more than I could stand. A pain stabbed at my heart. Was that possible?

I'd never believed in love at first sight any more than I really believed in God; I guess I thought they both existed. I wondered how I might have changed the way I led my life if those things had been a factor. Even in my elation I was sad. Les was right; maybe this was too much too soon. I chose to stay – and I'm glad I did.

I camped out in that booth for hours, engaging Monica in conversation as often as possible. I ordered more food than I could possibly eat just to get her to come back to my table. The half full plates piled up on the table.

With twinkling eyes she asked if I needed a box. I shook my head. Laughing, she cleared away the dishes. "All eyes and no stomach, eh?" She gave a wry smile and winked. Heat rose up my cheeks. "Either that, or you have a strange way of loitering." Her laugh held a magical and contagious quality, reminding me of a baby being tickled; you couldn't help but well up with joy.

Unable to find a way to extend my stay without ordering something else I couldn't eat, Monica dropped off the check. "I'm outta here. My shift's over." With a little prodding, I managed to convince her to sit with me for a while. We talked and laughed. When the laugh reached her dazzling light blue eyes, it was enough to melt my heart. Then she snorted and it was all over for the me sitting in the diner and the me observing from above. While live me almost rolled off the booth bench, dead me soared above, floating on a true high.

In that moment I fell in love with her. She stole both my human and ghostly hearts.

After a while, with reluctance Monica stood and said, "Oh, I haven't laughed that hard in I can't remember when. I do have to go though. It was nice meeting you. I had fun. Come back again sometime." She smiled, turned, and walked toward the door. My smile faded and my heart skipped a beat in panic. I didn't want this moment to end. Not ever. I urged myself to run after her. Fortunately, myself and I were of like minds.

CHAPTER

Six

Out on the street darkness had fallen. Something pulled at a memory string. Something important I had to do. When I caught sight of her, whatever the thought had been evaporated. Not wanting to scare her, I trotted, stopping short several feet behind her. Still, she stiffened as she heard my approach. Monica turned quick and stared at me hard. In her hand was a pepper spray canister. The look in her eyes left no doubt in my mind she wouldn't hesitate to use the burning spray.

I stopped and raised my hands. "I'm sorry. I shouldn't have run up on you like that. I-I," I didn't know what I. I lowered my hands and slid them in my back pockets. I looked down at the sidewalk as if there were cue cards written there to help me with my lines. When I looked up again Monica had relaxed a bit, but she still aimed the pepper spray in my direction.

I tried again. "I'm sorry for scaring you. Ah, can I walk you home?"

She cocked her head and narrowed her eyes at me.

"I just wanted to talk with you some more. I promise; when you want me to leave, say so and I'll be gone." I swung my arm sideways. "Besides, this is no neighborhood for a beautiful young woman like you to be walking home alone in the dark."

"I walk this way every night and have never had a problem before."

"Oh." I was at a loss for what to say next.

As I stared down at myself I wondered when I had become so wimpy. It was like a stranger resided in my body. Then Monica's eyes seemed to soften. "You can walk with me part way. But when I tell you to go, you go. Understood? If not, or if you try something stupid, I promise I'll blast you with my spray and kick you severely in the balls."

My hearts leaped in both bodies. Exhilaration surged through me unlike any I had ever known.

Monica was beautiful, smart, funny, and feisty. My earthen heart swelled and I stepped up next to her. She turned and began to walk. My corporal body felt light enough to float up to where I did.

"So Mr. Swift, tell me why I should allow you to walk with me."

"Uh, because I'm good company?"

"That remains to be seen. Tell me more."

My confidence grew. "Because I'm fun and I make you laugh."

"Oh really? Did it ever occur to you that I laughed just to be polite? You're not that funny."

Ouch!

Some of the confidence was slapped from my brain all the way up here. My real body visibly deflated. No wonder I never dated much. I was really bad at it.

Monica noticed my dejected posture and took pity on me. "I'm just kidding you. God, you're so easy to mess with. Believe me, if I wasn't having fun with you I never would've sat down and talked."

I relaxed and began to beam again. I knew that.

From that point we talked and laughed and got to know each other a little better. Being with her was glorious.

Preoccupied with her company, I lost track of how far we'd gone. Elation morphed into tension as the low murmur of voices came from the alley on our right.

Old training kicked in. My body sprung into defense mode. Muscles tightened; fists clenched. I peered into the darkness of the alley. The figures of three men came into view. As they emerged from the shadows I thought they might try to mug us, but they stopped at the edge of the alley and watched us pass by.

In an instant I was me again; eyes narrowed, scanning, analyzing the threat and the possible solutions like I'd been trained to do a lifetime ago and had done ever since. I was ready to defend in case they tried to attack from behind. Monica was so involved in telling a story about her first year in the city that she seemed oblivious to the men's presence.

My physical form couldn't relax until we'd put half a block between us and the three men. I watched from above, intending to give a warning should the men move, not thinking that any alarm would go unheard. One of the men struck a match. The flame moved to light a cigarette hanging from his lips, enlightening his face. I froze. A gut wrenching chill ran through me. Then anger grew and I wanted to kill.

This was one of the men who tracked, ambushed, and eventually killed me. How strange that he would be watching me in my most promising alternate life. Unfortunately, since on this world I was still alive, it meant this version of me didn't recognize him. *Damn!* Maybe this version didn't even exist.

As I raged within, I fell at a rapid descent. The distance between my killer and me diminished in the blink of an eye. Like Superman, I led fist first, driving into him. But I went right through his body, feeling no impact.

Coming out on the other side of the killer, I spun to face

my target. My confusion turned to blinding frustration, knowing now I could do nothing to hurt him. I swung at him anyway. I flailed non-stop with nothing to show for my efforts.

The man turned twice in my direction and scanned around as if looking for someone. I think he shivered once. That meant he could feel my presence if not my touch. My hope renewed, I attacked again, increasing my efforts.

I screamed and charged at him again. He turned toward his companions and the three men headed back down the alley. The tall wild-haired man exhaled a stream of gray smoke and said, “Man, that was some sweet piece.” He grabbed his crotch as he walked. “What I’d like to do with her.” The others laughed and added comments that faded away down the alley.

I watched him go until they were out of sight. Still angry, I looked around. My mind flashed to another alley showing a vivid portrayal of the place I'd made my final stand. The nagging thought from before returned exploding into a full-blown visual of my forgotten mission. *How long had I allowed myself to be sidetracked?* It was time to figure out a way back to life.

At the mouth of the alley, I looked to the right. Monica and I were two blocks away. Other me turned to look behind. For the briefest of moments I swore our eyes locked. I nodded. “*Don’t worry, brother; I got your back.*”

CHAPTER

Seven

Now, how to get back to my cloud? For that matter, I'd watched this thread for quite a while, but jumping out of it I had no idea where I was. Were there connectors somewhere, like on subway lines? I floated upward, still confused. "Hey, Les, can you hear me?" In a flash, Les' voice was in my head. "Picture where you want to go."

I did and was standing in my home. A second later Les joined me.

"Do you feel better now?" he asked.

"No!" I was angry. Agitated, I paced back and forth.

He gave a sad frown. "I did try to warn you. It's difficult sometimes to see where your life could have gone. I'm sorry. These threads are only possibilities though. You may never know what choice you might have made at the time to cause the branch to spring in another direction. Life's funny that way."

"Yeah, death's a stitch too," I said, my sarcasm thick. "But you said the thicker the thread, the more probable the choice, right?"

Les paused. He considered me for a moment and nodded, "Yes, but …"

"Les, I have to go back. I can help so many people. Please; just long enough to make things right."

"No matter how badly you want to or how hard you try, you'll never be able to physically touch anyone on earth. There is no way to go back to life –no way to make contact.

It's set up that way for a reason. But Chance, listen to me. Even if I wanted to send you back, I don't have the power. Asking me is a waste of breath."

I sighed. "I see that, but I had to try. I saw a man in that thread. He was one of the men who killed me. That means whatever they were planning hasn't happened yet or that they got away with it. Lives are at stake here; lots of lives."

"As they are every day on earth. A long time ago I gave up watching events on earth that cause so much pain to so many. I could do nothing to alter the outcome, so why watch the suffering?"

"But you don't understand. Man, I was so close. I wasn't supposed to lose. How did it happen? I was winning. I-I..." I stared at my closed fists. "I failed."

Les didn't respond.

Putting my hands on top of my head I turned in a circle, wracking my brain for a solution. "I need to see my death. I want to know how those killers took me down."

"You might not want to do that. Seeing your own demise can sometimes be very traumatic. I've seen it destroy spirits and haunt the dead for a long time. The vision of watching yourself be killed can haunt you, literally, for an eternity. It's no way to spend your afterlife."

"But I have to understand what happened. Maybe then I can find some way to stop whatever the horrible event is they have planned."

"You don't even know for sure a threat exists, Chance."

"My gut tells me the danger is real. I trusted my instincts for years and they have never let me down. It's real and inside, deep inside, my gut's telling me there's still time and I can do something about it."

Les shook his head. "The truth is that it's nothing more

than your desire for it to be real and that this is fantasy. I'm sorry, but the sooner you come to grips with the reality of your situation, the sooner you'll be able to enjoy what you have here and perhaps move on to your final reward."

I sneered. "Do you think I'm the type of person who could relax and enjoy eternity knowing I failed to save the lives of so many people?" I was shouting now. "No, if I can't fix this you might as well destroy my spirit now, because my soul will already be gone."

Taking deep unnecessary breaths, the rage within in me began to subside. Now was not the time for anger; that would come later, should I succeed. Right now I needed a sharp, calculating mind. "I'm gonna find a way." The calmness and confidence in my voice surprised me but helped me realize I wouldn't give up until I did find a way.

"You can dream about it, think about it, try to plan for it, or make an emotional plea, but you don't have a ghost of a chance of making it back to life. I'm sorry. No matter how great your desire or how pure your purpose, it can't be done. Believe me, everyone tries; even me."

CHAPTER

Eight

I lifted my head and gaped at Les. "You tried?"

"It's true. It was many years ago, but I exhausted all possible options. When I finally came to terms with the reality of the situation, I was much more accepting. Now I never think about it, and you know what? I'm perfectly happy and quite content."

"But that's you. I'm not like you. I have to at least try."

Les said, "I do understand. I wish I could convince you how futile it is, but I do understand."

"No, I don't think you do. I was sitting in a restaurant and overheard a conversation about a bomb being detonated somewhere in the city. Three men," I swallowed the rising anger, "three terrorists laughed about the thousands they hoped to kill. One of them passed a flash drive to the other two. He said it contained the schematics, the arming codes, and the location where the bomb was to be placed. The bomb was scheduled to go off four days from then. Then he left, leaving the other two sipping their drinks and chatting like it was just another normal day."

My pacing increased in speed; my arms became more animated.

"I couldn't let them get away with mass murder. I called the police but before I could talk to someone the men got up and walked out. I couldn't let them get away. Following them, I tried to stay inconspicuous while talking in a whisper to the 911 operator. In a hurry, I relayed what I'd heard: that terrorists planned on detonating a bomb somewhere in the city. I explained I was tailing two of the terrorists, but she wouldn't believe me because I wouldn't give her my name and they could get no read from the phone I used.

"As much as I wanted to help, I couldn't tell her who I was. I had a record and they might not have taken me seriously; even worse, they might have come after me. I couldn't risk it, so I disconnected and decided to handle it myself."

Les interrupted then. "Perhaps that decision was where your thread branched, driving you toward this conclusion."

I stopped pacing and frowned at Les. "Yeah, thanks for that input, Captain Obvious." Continuing, I said, "When the two men turned a corner, I rushed them from behind, bowling them over." I paused as an important thought began to burrow up from the other facts. Something wasn't right; well, a lot of things weren't right, actually, but this was important. I spoke my thoughts, no longer talking to Les. "If I had gotten away with no pursuit, how the hell did they find me?"

The story became alive again as I relayed it. It was like watching a movie of my life. "The two men went sprawling. I kicked one, and then dropped on the second man who had the flash drive. My fist exploded against his head." The sounds came alive in my mind. The smack of hard bone meeting soft flesh. "His head bounced off the cement; his eyes unfocused.

"My hands dove into his pockets until I found the flash drive. I snatched it and turned to make my escape, but the other thug grabbed my leg and fumbled a gun out from behind his back." I froze that scene for a second, trying to recall if I'd missed anything. Perhaps something I'd gleaned in my periphery and stored in my subconscious, but no. I continued.

"I stomped on him," I told Les, "and kicked the gun away. Then I ran for all I was worth.

"The two men did not follow. I ducked around the corner of a building and peered back. One man was on a cell phone, gesticulating wildly. The other man stood holding his bleeding face. They were panicked, adding to my suspicions that whatever was on the flash drive was the real deal."

I stopped talking, allowing the mental movie to play on. I was about to duck away when I noticed the bleeding man stoop to pick up something on the ground. And there it was: a piece of paper. I hadn't been aware of it then. My hands dug into my pockets. I pulled them each inside out and came up empty. The realization hit me then. Of all the dumb luck! "They got my name from the credit card slip that had fallen from my pocket."

CHAPTER

Nine

Neither Les nor I spoke for quite a while. When I snapped out of my fugue and focused my eyes again, I was back on my little cloud cell. The picture of my platoon still hung in midair.

"If I hadn't been at that restaurant I wouldn't have heard those men talking. If I didn't follow them… If I would've just let it alone or let the police handle it… I'd…"

"You can second guess the decisions that led you down that final road all you want, but it's not going to change anything. And besides, to not make those choices would have been out of character for you."

"But I'd still be alive and—and I'd be with Monica."

"But could you have lived with yourself if you had done nothing and the bomb went off?"

"I *did* do something and the bomb *still is* gonna go off. Only now I'm dead and I never had the chance to meet Monica." Anguished, I swallowed hard and said, "Even if we both would've died in the blast, at least we would've had those few moments."

Les rested a comforting arm across my shoulders. "I'm very sorry, Chance. It's never been said that life was fair. Perhaps in time you will find a bChancece here that makes it right. We can never know the ultimate plan. If we truly believe that God has a plan or works in mysterious ways, then we must take comfort in the fact that after a while all things are made right." He dropped his arm.

"I don't know if that helps or if you think it's all gibberish, but it's all I've got. It's what I've embraced with all my heart. I have no choice but to believe it for myself."

He shrugged and left me then, vanishing like the ghost he was. I guess he figured he had done all he could for me. His advice lingered for a time. But then, as if snapping awake from a deep sleep, I shook off his words like a bad dream. *No, God Damn it*! Sorry, but I wasn't quitting. It was time for Swifty to get to work and do what he was good at – fixing people's problems.

After a long glance at the picture of my old squad mates, I cleared my mind and began organizing the little information I had. It was, in fact, sparse. I didn't know much but I was buoyed by the knowledge I'd started with less before and got the job done. Of course, being alive made it easier to collect useful information, but as I'd been taught, it was time to adapt to the situation.

First things first; how did they keep track of time around here? How much time had gone by since I started thread hopping?

Somehow the answer appeared in my brain. I had lost an entire day. Less than three days remained before the bomb was set to explode. No matter what Les said, I was going to try with every fiber of my somewhat translucent being. If I had been willing to die trying to help when alive, I wouldn't let death stop me now.

CHAPTER

Ten

"He put up a hellauva fight, that's for sure," forensic pathologist Cyndi Bartz said, peering over the top of her magnifying glass at the young detective standing in her exam room.

First year detective Michael Pollen pretended to jot something on his notepad to avoid gaping at the dissected body.

Bartz continued. "His knuckles are bruised and scraped. There was blood on his hands and shirt that may not be his. There are several cuts on his arms, probably from a knife."

"That matches what we found at the crime scene," Pollen said, scribbling again. "We took blood samples from a lot of different spots. He may have made his attackers bleed."

"Attackers?" Bartz looked up, eyebrows raised.

"There were at least two, maybe more."

"Well he couldn't fight the bullet. Someone planted one in the back of his head." She gestured to a small metal pan. "A .22 from fairly close. He was dead before he hit the ground." Bartz continued to work, talking without looking at the detective. "So, Mike, you figure out who he was yet?"

Pollen nodded. "Yeah. Prints came back as Chance R. Swift. Age 31. Spent time in the Rangers; got a coupla medals. Saved some lives in the war. Great service record. Known as a go-to guy, someone who could get a difficult job done."

He flipped a page. "What's interesting is there's no

verifiable means of financial support." He glanced at the body. The physique was one Pollen wished he had time for. There were no tell-tale needle tracks or other signs to suggest Swift had been a druggie, and from what he'd been able to find out so far, didn't appear to be a man who would've been dealing anyway.

Then again, there were all kinds of things to deal in this world. So many ex-vets had fallen into illegal activities to support themselves. Their skill set only left them qualified for a few jobs. "Got a record, too. Beat some guy up who was physically abusing his wife."

"He should have got a medal for that, too."

"Yeah, but like many cases, the wife refused to file charges against her husband or to support Swift's actions, so he got busted for assault."

Bartz paused for a moment and studied the body. "He sure was built. With his training I could see how it would take a few to take him down."

"Anyone can take down the toughest man in the world. It only takes one bullet."

Bartz grunted her agreement and resumed her work. "So you thinking mugging and he resisted?"

"I guess it was something like that, except he still had his wallet with a coupla hundred in cash inside. Maybe he messed his assailants up so much that they left without robbing him. We'll see what the blood turns up. Oh, and the tooth."

Bartz stopped again and stared open-mouthed at Pollen. "He knocked out a tooth?"

"Yep. Suppose I'll have to put out an alert to all the dentists and oral surgeons in the city."

Pollen slid the notebook inside his jacket pocket.

"Anything else?"

"Not really. He was healthy. No signs of drug or alcohol abuse. Lots of small scars, including two previous bullet wounds. He led a physically active life."

"Yeah, he was a war hero. But look where it got him." He headed for the door. "I'll wait for the reports. Talk to you later, Cyndi."

"Bye." She watched him go using her magnified glasses to study his body. She sighed and returned to her work.

Pollen headed back to the police station, his mind churning as he walked. What had happened to Chance Swift? Was it as simple as a robbery? His wallet had close to two hundred dollars in it. Robbery didn't seem likely, but if his attackers had their hands full they may have shot Swift then fled the scene without checking. His gut told him the muggers were lucky to be able to walk away. If one of them hadn't had a gun it might have gone an entirely different way.

Mr. Swift, what have you been doing with yourself since you got out of the service? He certainly didn't look like he was living on the streets or on welfare. Pending the reports, there wasn't much to do. He would attempt to find where he lived, starting with the address on his license. If that was a dead end, he wasn't sure where to go with it. He had other much more promising cases to work on.

He'd give this case twenty-four hours' worth of his attention before sliding it to the bottom of his caseload pile. He would have to check the files and look for similar attacks, but Pollen had a feeling this one was going to go unsolved.

CHAPTER

Eleven

I sat on a lawn chair I had conjured from my memory. My elbows rested on my knees; my chin was cradled in my hands. My gaze had glazed over from staring out into the emptiness. I was barely aware of the darkness that surrounded me.

I had been able to clear away the veil of clouds and look down on earth. From this heavenly perch I searched for an answer, but none came and according to Les, this wasn't heaven. Perhaps my interpretation of heaven was based too heavily on earthly perceptions as to what life after death would be like. We always picture our spirits or guardian angels hovering above.

My attempts at piecing together what I did and didn't know had stalled quite a while ago. No matter how I looked at the situation, I was at a loss. I stared outward in an endless trance, hoping for some final puzzle piece to fall into place and give me a clue as to the direction I should take.

I wasn't ready to admit that going back was looking hopeless, but it was getting close. Clearing my mind to take a break, I sucked in a deep breath, if only because it made me feel like I was still alive. I needed a blank canvas on which to paint the faint picture I envisioned from a different perspective.

In the distance below my position, I saw what looked like a shooting star. A few seconds later I saw another. My curiosity piqued, I raised my head up and swept the earthly horizon from left to right. It was like a meteor shower. The lights shot up and left small tails behind, blazed across the night sky, and disappeared into space. Each tail lasted different lengths of time before gradually fading from sight. Some were long, some short; some faint, while others were thick and bright.

"Hey, Les?" I called out. I spun around, looking over my shoulders. Nothing. Huh! Maybe he was like a genie and I'd used up my free wishes. "Calling Les – yo, soul mate – you out there somewhere?"

He appeared then and looked irritated. "Don't call me that. I'm a guide – someone to help you on your journey. I'm not your servant. If you have questions I can help with I'm here for you, but please, no more about going back, okay?

I shrugged. "Sure." I would just have to ask without asking. I pointed toward the light show. "What are those?"

"I see you're learning how things work. I assume you're talking about the streaks. Those are souls leaving their bodies."

I watched for a moment, amazed. "Wow! So they blast off to the heavens like shooting stars? Did I do that too?"

Les, smiled. "Yes, we all do."

"Wow! It looks like a lot of people are dying. Is that normal?"

"You have to remember how many people are on earth. What you're seeing is actually a very small percentage of that population."

I watched a while longer before something clicked. "It gets dark here?"

"It can."

"So there's day and night?"

"There can be."

I shot Les my best exasperated look. "Do you ever give a complete answer?"

He smiled. "Sometimes."

I grunted, tired of that annoying smile.

"Your mind is operating like you're still alive. Your brain automatically created day and night because that's what it's programmed for. Most people keep that time allocation, until they understand time no longer matters. Some use all night, some all day. This is your world; you choose."

I sighed. "I guess I'll leave it the way I'm used to for now." The darkness had accomplished one thing: it had increased my depression. "I think you've been misleading me."

"How's that?"

"I think this is actually hell. It's boring here. I'm so bored, if I wasn't already dead, I'd kill myself. There's nothing to do here but sit and stare. I can't stand it."

Les studied me. For a brief moment I thought I saw his eyes move through a series of emotions from concern to regret to pity. As quickly as the look came, it was gone.

"There are plenty of things to do to occupy your time. You just haven't searched for or created anything yet. What did you enjoy doing when you were alive? You know; hobbies, interests, sports... that type of thing."

I gave it some thought. "I was a big baseball fan. In fact, I played a little minor league ball before going into the service."

"Well, if you like baseball, you can get up a game anytime you want. There's lot of major and minor league ballplayers here. I'm sure there's always a game going on. You'd be surprised by who you could play with."

In spite of my growing angst, my eyebrows raised in interest. I did love baseball. I played it for as long as I could before age and lack of time forced me to give it up. “You mean like Ruth and Gehrig and DiMaggio?”

“Well, one of them is still here and many others as well. You just have to want to play and you will find a game somewhere.”

“Mantle?”

“Of course.”

“Jackie Robinson?”

“No, he's moved up to the majors.”

I hesitated a moment, then understood. He was no longer in the undecided category, like me.

“Cobb?”

“No. He... ah... didn’t make the team.” Les smirked.

“Oh.” Then I laughed.

“That could be fun. I’d love to play again.” But even as the words left my mouth, a pang of guilt swept over me. As fun as playing baseball with all-time greats would be, I still had important things to do. I couldn’t allow myself to be distracted again. I’d already lost one day and I had to keep looking for an answer.

Once more I lowered my head, distraught. I could do nothing to save those people or Monica. I had less than three days to figure something out. If Les, who had been here much longer than me, couldn’t find a way to gain his life back, I didn’t know why I thought I could.

CHAPTER

Twelve

As I stared out into the infinite darkness, a twinkle lit the sky down by earth. I watched and it happened again. Over the next half hour the light flashed several more times, but not with any regularity. It reminded me of someone turning a flashlight on and off real fast, as if signaling a code over a long distance.

"What's that?" I pointed when the light flashed.

"That is a soul who has not died yet, someone whose death has not yet been assured."

"You mean like someone who's been shot and is bleeding out?"

"No, because they are technically still alive until they're not. In this case, it is most likely someone who is in a coma. Their body may have shut down but their mind is still alive. They keep fighting the pull of eternity's promise, afraid to give up life for the finality of death."

"Ah."

"Or maybe God hasn't decided if He's done with them yet." He shrugged. "Who knows?"

I rolled my eyes. "Thanks, you're a big help."

"Hey, you asked."

A light bulb brightened in my head. "Wait, does that mean they have contact with both worlds?"

"Yes, I guess that's one way of looking at it, but—oh, wait—I know what you're thinking. Sorry, but it doesn't work that way. In theory, it's a good thought, but you just can't enter into someone else's life force."

"Why not? What about all those stories about near death experiences where someone comes back to life and tells stories about seeing the other side? There has to be some basis in reality. Too many of stories have been recorded like that to discount them as imagination."

Les shook his head. "More likely, that individual pulled the thought of contact from a buried memory in their subconscious. There's never been any true scientific evidence. It's just ghost chasing. People believe because they refuse to let go, to give up hope."

"You mean like me?"

He smiled and this time it was genuine. "Yeah, like you, although I have to say, the strength of your determination surprises me."

"But, Les," I stood, excited, knocking the lightweight chair over. I looked at it, annoyed. Without me touching it, the chair righted itself. "In theory, you have to admit there has to be a possibility. I mean, if so many people have said the same thing over centuries and in different parts of the world and have had no prior contact with or knowledge of others who have had similar experiences, then there must be some truth to their stories. Don't you think? I mean, speaking perfectly theoretically here."

"There is no such thing as perfect theories or they would stop being theories."

"See, you agree." It was my turn to smile.

"Huh?"

"Oh, work with me here, Les. In theory, there has to be something to near death experiences. If you can't prove it, you also can't disprove it."

A low growl came from his throat. He was either hungry

or I was starting to get to him. "In essence, I suppose you could communicate with them. In theory. But that light you see is their life force and penetrating it is impossible. That individual wouldn't know you and certainly wouldn't let down their guard to admit you. Besides that, to do so may end their life, so it wouldn't matter or help. You could be responsible for killing someone who still had a chance to survive. You could be the reason a branch sprouts from their intended thread."

My face must have betrayed my thoughts because he waved me off. "Oh now, hold on a second, Chance. We're just talking theory here. There is no foundation there to build from."

He was irritated with me but I had him on the ropes and was winning the round. I pressed on.

"I'm good at building things. Besides, isn't it written somewhere, 'God helps those who help themselves'?"

"Careful, Chance. Now you're twisting sacred words to fit your needs. Remember while you are here, you're scoring points that will determine where your soul ends up for eternity."

I whirled on him then with exploding anger. "Do you really think I wouldn't sacrifice my eternal soul to save those people? To have the chance to save the woman I might have married in another life? In the heartbeat I no longer have, I would!"

Les turned away from me and rubbed a hand over his head.

"Les, I'm sorry I yelled. I know this isn't your fault. I'm not blaming you. I-I can't help how I am. I have to do this. I have to find a way. If I fail and those people die, well, at least I tried. But if I sit here and watch as they die and make no effort at all, well, I'll never find peace, no matter how long eternity is. It's part of who I am. Maybe it was the only good part, but I can't give it up. Can you understand that?"

With perhaps the most crestfallen expression I'd ever seen, Les whispered in an anguished voice, "Yes, I can."

CHAPTER

Thirteen

The silence that settled over us was painful, and yet I sensed for the first time that I had an ally. I'd made my argument and all I could do now was wait.

"Chance, let's stop for a second and look at the facts. First; you are deceased and that is a living soul. Second; what you are suggesting has never been done before and, in all likelihood cannot be, and third; even if somehow you did make contact there would be no way of communicating with anyone else if the body lies in a coma.

"Regardless, it's worth exploring."

"Oh, for God's, er, heaven's sake. Chance, think about what you're suggesting. Do you really think someone hasn't thought about doing what you want to attempt? If they had been successful, every spirit throughout the ages would be assaulting the near living by trying to send back messages. Somewhere checks and balances have been put into place to protect those souls locked between two worlds."

"Look, it's the only opportunity that's presented itself so far. How do I get to him?"

"Chance…"

"Les, I have to try. Please help me. I can't let this go, not if there's a 'ghost of a chance,' as you put it. I have to do this. How do I get there?" Les looked at me and nodded. "I know you can't resist thinking about the possibility, but I'm trying to spare you the angst if you can't get through. It's a lot like international calling. You might place the call, but it doesn't mean anyone on the other side can hear you."

"But at least I will have tried."

Les looked at me for a moment, silent. Then he sighed. "Very well; if you won't take my word for it, then it's best that you find out for yourself. Maybe that way you'll be disappointed, but you'll see the reality of your situation and be able to better accept it."

"Les," I said.

"What?"

"Less talk, more action."

"Funny."

I blinked, and when I reopened my eyes, I found myself in what appeared to be a room in some kind of private medical care facility. A body, looking more like a mummy than a man, lay on the bed. Numerous leads and lines hung from various monitors and were attached to the body.

A man and two women sat around the bed. Sandra, the patient's mother, sat to the right of the bed. She was a large woman with dark disheveled hair piled high, but not fashionably, with loose ends sticking out everywhere. The father, Barney, a tall slender man, sat on the end of the bed. His face was ashen; his eyes were fixed and unseeing. He looked to be in a state of shock.

On the left side of the bed sat Caroline, the victim's fiancée. She was pretty and slightly plump with short auburn hair that framed her face. Her deep blue eyes were swimming in tears that made long black tracks down her round cheeks. One of her hands was intertwined with the hands of the unresponsive patient, Garrett MacIntosh—Mac to his friends.

How I knew any of their names was a complete surprise to me and beyond my current level of understanding.

Mac was a sight reminiscent of some horror movie. His head was completely swathed in bandages, leaving only his eyes and mouth and a small opening for his nostrils uncovered. His left arm and both legs were encased from top to bottom in casts. It hurt me just to look at him. I could only imagine the pain he must have endured before being chased to the safety of the coma. I didn't want to know the damage that had been done to his body or the grisly details that had put him on that bed. In fact, with cold detachment, I didn't want to know any more about him than necessary. He was the means to an end; nothing more.

Les had informed me I wouldn't be able to see his past or any possible threads. The only part of his life I could witness was the present as it happened. That was the part that interested me anyway.

A doctor entered the room. All three visitors lifted their heads to watch him. With a grim expression on his face, he spoke a few reassuring words and then departed. The lost looks returned to their faces.

Over the next hour I hovered above, observed, and listened. From their conversations, I pieced together that Mac had been in a motorcycle accident. He was, in fact, lucky to be alive. He flew over the hood of a car that had turned unexpectedly in front of him. Mac landed on his back and cracked his head on the concrete street. Although he was wearing a helmet, it had split wide open upon impact. The second and all consequent bounces had only the skull to protect the brain.

Mac had many other injuries as well, but the life-threatening one was the blow to the head. Since the accident, Mac had remained unresponsive. The doctor had little confidence in a recovery but in the event it should occur, warned that the most likely outcome would be severe and permanent physical and probably mental damage.

Currently Mac was on life support. His chest rose and fell with the aid of machines. At this point, Mac was day to day. Each hour that passed brought new hope, although the doctor had just broached the subject of knowing when it would be time to pull the plug. That, of course, was too much for the family to think about. It was far too early and they still had hope that Mac would open his eyes and return to them. Although from the sound of things, that was like praying for a miracle.

I watched from a corner of the room. Caroline's tears flowed in an unending stream. Sandra reached out to her but withdrew her hand, knowing there was no comfort she could offer as she was having emotional issues of her own. Barney continued to stare at his son's form, refusing to believe this was the end.

Although I was only a ghost or spirit or whatever, the pain and emotion that hung over the room was so thick I could feel it, or at least imagined I could. It would have been easy to get caught up in the suffering, but emotions would be unproductive to my objectives so I walled them out. Even so, I wished there was some way to help them ... maybe there was.

I walked forward and put my hand on Garrett's undamaged arm. Nothing happened. I'm not sure what I expected; an instant connection or maybe a spark? I should have known making contact wouldn't be that simple. Now what? I floated toward Garrett's wrapped head. Maybe I could enter his brain. Instead I passed right through him and wound up standing on the floor. If Mac could have seen me I don't think he would have appreciated where his mouth was in relationship to my body.

I floated upward and hovered around the ceiling. I had to admit that the floating and flying part of being dead was pretty cool. I studied Mac while trying to form some sort of entry strategy. There had to be a way to make contact. I tried speaking to him but figured out real fast nothing was connecting. Maybe because he wasn't dead yet he was unable to hear me, but if he was dead, he was of no use to me.

CHAPTER

Fourteen

Mac's father unfolded himself from the uncomfortable looking chair. He grunted from the effort tearing me from my thoughts. I watched as he shuffled zombie-like out of the room. A sob from the mother followed him out, which started Caroline crying again. The scene had become too distracting. I had to get out of there and attack the problem from a different angle.

Back home I sat in my lawn chair and studied the ever wavering flicker of Mac's life force. Could the light that shown toward the heavens be my way in? If that was his spirit trying to leave his body, perhaps that was my point of contact.

Descending to a point directly over Mac's body, I waited, but no flashlight beam came. There was no sign of a spirit light at all. Confusion built and with it frustration began to climb. What was I missing?

I climbed higher equal to the height of my cloud. I stopped and looked down. From this height the soul lights were visible. Focusing with all my attention, I scanned the atmosphere for any sign of Mac. Nothing.

For several maddening minutes I waited. Perhaps Mac was healing and no longer on the verge of death. Good for him, but extremely bad for me and for the thousands that would perish in the explosion.

The same problem would occur if he already died and

passed by me before I noticed. I zoomed back to his room. There didn't appear to be any change. Mac still lay motionless. His loved ones still clung to their hopes and prayers and the machines continued their constant blinking, dinging, and hissing.

Racing back skyward, I stopped and waited. This time the flash pulsed very fast, on-off, but the beam of light was weak and growing dimmer. I wasn't sure what that meant, but doubted it was good. Then it winked out.

Keeping my eyes pinpointed on the spot where I had seen the light, I began a slow descent. I thought I was directly above the light, but couldn't be sure until- and if- it beamed again. If I had a physical body, it would have been filled with tension. Had this much time passed between bursts of light when I watched from my cloud?

Mac's life light flashed again. I dove for it but it vanished before I reacted. I would have to wait and try again. I wanted to scream away my frustration but held it in. My heart pounded faster. The beating wasn't real, but it was what I might have expected had I been alive. I let it go unchecked. After all, it wasn't like I had to worry about my blood pressure now.

Drifting down a little closer, I was fairly certain I was right on top of the light now. To ease my tension I took long deep breaths. It worked on earth when I was getting ready to confront someone, either on the street or in Afghanistan. Obviously I didn't need to breathe now, but the steady routine helped calm me.

The minutes ticked by. Despite my breathing exercises, the strain magnified. It was like being in a batting cage and trying to time between pitches. Sometimes you grew so anxious waiting that you jumped at the pitch, striding too early and taking a weak swing, which was what happened. The light flashed and I jumped. This time I just caught the tail end of the narrow beam. It hit me like a battering ram, sending me rocketing through space.

I'm not sure how long it took for me to stop, but I was a long way from home. I looked around to see if anyone was watching; you know the way you do when you've done something so embarrassing the act had to be witnessed by someone. Was there a ghost version of YouTube I'd be appearing on?

Descending again I found Mac's power hammer and followed it down. I could not so much touch it as sense its form. No matter what I tried—angle, force, or both—my hand would not penetrate. Backing away, I regrouped. Without knowing why, since I'd had no success so far, the thought came to me that I was onto something.

The light faded again. I flew above and waited. This time, as it reignited, I stayed just beyond its reach. I was relieved when it stopped short of me, not only because it hit like a cosmic cement truck, but also if Mac had died, his soul would have passed straight through me.

Once more the light faded. Mac must be fighting very hard to hold on to life. I rooted for him to make it, but just not yet.

I thought about the light beam. If I was at the top of the beam when it hit and propelled me, maybe I needed to be down farther when it pulsed. Maybe if I were inside the circumference it would envelop me. Yeah; then what? I'd be trapped inside someone else's life. More like, I'd be spit out like a giant ball of phlegm splattering someplace on the other side of the universe. Either way, I would learn from the attempt and try something different the next time. Trial and error. Besides, what did it matter if I were trapped or pummeled?

With a gauge for the distance now, fully realizing that it could change, I lowered to a point about halfway down from what I remembered the height to be. Then, I waited – and waited some more. "Come on Garrett," I shouted, "work with me here."

Without warning the flash came; bright but not blinding. I closed my eyes against the impact. A loud whoosh surrounded me. Then, with a strangled cry escaping my mouth, the beam pulled me earthward at an incredible speed.

In a blink I was inside a small room; a small gooey, gray room. Someone else was there, but clouded in a haze my eyes could not penetrate. I looked around, wondering what the hell happened. What light there was pulsated from the walls of the strange cell. Edging closer, I studied the walls. They were a lumpy assortment of various shades of gray. Thin channels ran between the lumps, carrying a multitude of iridescent threads that flashed with what looked like electric current.

Wait! Gray and gooey? Electrical charges? Understanding hit me like a bolt of lightning. I had reached the confines of Mac's brain.

CHAPTER

Fifteen

As I watched with ever-widening eyes, a healthy but frazzled-looking Garrett MacIntosh stepped from the mist. We stared at each other with mouths agape.

"Are you here for me?"

He spoke. And I heard him. I was too amazed and excited to answer.

"Is it over, then?" He gasped, and my elation turned to uncertainty. He stared at my face. Was my bullet wound showing? My hands probed my head for a hole.

"Oh my God, you're taking me to hell, aren't you?" he dropped to his knees and began sobbing and pleading. "I'm sorry, God! I tried to be good!"

I realized then I must have appeared demonic to his already stressed psyche. I held up both hands, waving them up and down as if guiding a plane to its landing strip. "Hey, hey, Garrett, easy, buddy. I'm not here to take you anywhere."

"You're not? You're not here for me?" He sat back on his haunches, a confused look spreading across his slender face. "I don't understand. Why are you here, to prepare me – like a ghost priest or something?"

"I am here for you, just not in the way you think."

"Does that mean I'm dead?"

I used the hands again. He wiped his eyes and stood. "No, no, not yet. Well, I—wait, let me back up and explain. I need your help. I need to get a message to someone."

"What? Who are you, and why am I seeing you?" His eyes widened and he took a step back.

I tried to control my excitement and slow down. "My name's Swift. I'm dead, you're not." The words had a sudden, dizzying effect on me. I'd never actually said the words before. I was really dead. This wasn't a conversation between two living beings. One was dead and one almost dead. I felt sick. Ironically, I think I turned pale. If that was possible.

"Hey, you all right?"

His words stabilized me for the moment. Whatever I was feeling, getting my message out was more important than me spewing ghost vomit.

"I guess that's a dumb question if you're already dead," Garrett said.

I took a step closer and met his eyes. "Garrett, I desperately need your help. A lot of people are going to die if I don't get word to someone on earth."

Distracted by something behind me, Garrett looked over my shoulder. I glanced back and saw a brightly lit tunnel. My eyes widened first in surprise, then in shock. What had once been my heart froze in panic.

"Oh God, no! Not yet!"

I spun on Garrett and tried to block his view. However, he had seen the light and it was already having a hypnotic effect.

"Garrett." No response. "Garrett!" I yelled. I lunged toward him, grabbing his shoulders, and was surprised when I could feel him. I shook him to break the hold the light had on him. "You don't want to go near the light. If you enter the light it means you are dead."

He smiled, still transfixed. "But it's so beautiful. I feel so warm."

I didn't remember seeing a light. Maybe I died so fast I needed no encouragement. Maybe the light was only there to entice those near death to take the final step and let go of their bodies. I was too new to the process to understand.

What I did understand, however, was that if he stepped into that light, any chance I had of saving those innocent people would be gone. Was I being selfish? Perhaps. Maybe it wasn't fair that I was trying to deny Garrett's entrance into eternity. But hell, the name alone should have told him it didn't matter when he got there, it was forever anyway.

So, wrong or right, I was going to steer him away from the light. I shook him again harder and got in his face. Then I played my ace.

"Garrett, do you want to be dead or alive? Think of your fiancée Caroline. Wouldn't you like to hold her again?"

I know I hadn't been dead long, but any points I'd accumulated so far were surely just erased.

CHAPTER

Sixteen

A sad and distant expression came over his face. "Caroline." His voice was soft and unsteady. Tears began to roll down his cheeks. I felt guilty playing with his emotions like that, but at least it stopped him from his journey to the really north country.

I spoke fast, the words slightly ahead of my thought process. "Caroline misses you. She needs you. She's in the room now, crying over your body. You can't leave her alone. You'll break that poor girl's heart."

If I wasn't going to hell before, the ticket was surely being printed now.

"Can you help me get back to her?" A pleading whine had entered his voice.

"I don't know, but I'll try if you will. I'm betting a lot of your recovery will have to do with how hard you fight to stay alive. Are you up to it?"

"Yeah, I want to see Caroline."

"Ah, I should tell you that your mom and dad are there too. They're all very upset about your condition."

"You can see them?"

"Yes, but I can't talk to them."

Garrett squinted and contorted his face like he had to go to the bathroom. "I can't see them. Are they close to me?"

"Yes. Caroline is holding your hand."

"Why can't I feel her?"

"You're in a coma. Your mind has shut down to control

the pain while your body tries to heal. Your injuries are quite severe though. It's going to take some effort."

"Oh." He seemed to give that thought. "So I really could die then, huh?"

"Yeah, I'm sorry."

"We were going to be married in a few months. I may never see her again. They're right about life being too short, you know?"

I winced. "Yeah brother, I hear you there."

"Wow, this is really sad."

I thought I was gonna lose him there. His body sagged and tears flowed anew. He covered his eyes with his hands.

"Look, Garrett, I wasn't kidding about needing your help. I'm not even sure it will work, but this is a desperate situation. I have to get word to someone, anyone, who can stop these guys from setting off a bomb."

He blinked fast a few times. I almost expected to hear that whirring sound a computer makes as his brain attempted to process what I'd said. "A bomb? Really? Like terrorists?"

"Yeah, I guess." I gave a hurried explanation and then pressed him hard. Will you try? It might even give you a chance to see Caroline again." I bit my tongue hard from guilt and to punish myself for playing his emotions so blatantly. The fact that I couldn't feel the pain did not matter.

He got excited. "Sure I will if I can see her one more time. What do you want me to do?"

"I'm not sure. Maybe you need to open up a portion of your mind and try to speak. You know, like opening up a portal between your subconscious and conscious minds. See if you can say 'bomb'."

"Just 'bomb'?"

I shrugged. "I'm new at this too. Let's see if it works. If

you can speak I'll give you more direction."

"Okay. How do I start?"

I was so consumed with making initial contact I hadn't given reentry much thought. But if he still had a chance of surviving his injuries, then there had to be a way back, right? "Try thinking it. Just picture yourself back in your body.

"Okay, I guess I can try. I'm ready when you are."

"Hold on a second. Let me get back to the room." I had the thought and the next instant I was in the corner of the Mac's hospital room. Nothing had changed much. Caroline had her head on Garrett's unhurt arm, still holding his hand. Sandra was sitting staring out the window, her lips moving in silent prayer. Barney was looking at the floor between his feet.

I watched and waited, growing more anxious as each second passed. I was beginning to think nothing was going to happen when Caroline lifted her head and gazed at Garrett. *This is it!* Anticipation built to the point of exploding me in tiny ghost-like particles all over the room. She must have felt something. I studied Mac's lips to detect movement, but they didn't move.

Caroline wiped her tears, stood up, and left the room.

"Wait!" I yelled. "You can't leave now! Garrett's trying to contact you!"

Like an idiot, I wasted several seconds trying to grasp the door latch before remembering I had no physical form. I slipped through the closed door and followed Caroline down the hall. She went into the ladies bathroom and I did too. She stopped in front of a mirror and examined her tear-streaked face, but she made no effort to wipe them away.

"Caroline!" I called. "Caroline!" I shouted louder, hoping her lack of response had to do with my volume. "You have to go back. Mac is trying to contact you."

She gave no indication as to having heard. Instead, she closed her eyes and her lips began to move in what I could only assume was yet another silent prayer. I wanted to say more, but when she made for the toilet, I gave up. She wasn't going to hear me anyway. Disappointed, I left, upset and desperate for the solution to the problem to jump out at me.

Back in Mac's room, his body still lay motionless, as were his folks. I sighed, disheartened. If he'd said anything while I was out, his parents would've been animated to the point of doing cartwheels. I should've known making contact wouldn't have been that easy.

Instead of jumping into Mac's mind through his essence, I tried to go straight into his head from the room. It didn't work. It took several minutes before I could catch his light and ride the beam back to him.

Mac was lounging on a sofa watching an old-style TV. "What happened?" I said, throwing my hands up in the air.

"I tried, but nothing happened."

"How hard did you try?"

He shot me an irritated look. "Hey, I tried. It didn't work."

"Man!"

CHAPTER

Seventeen

I wished I could trade places with him. Frustration caused my anger to boil over. "Did you really open up your mind? That girl out there needs to hear from you! I doubt you love her one tenth what she loves you. If she was here instead of you, I know she'd try. She wouldn't let you or thousands of people get blown up."

"Stop it. Don't even say that about Caroline being here instead of me! I wouldn't want that for her. You stop talking like that or I'll kick your ass."

"Yeah? Bullshit. You'd have to put out some effort to do that and that would be too much work for a lazy ass like you."

I was never afraid to fight; actually, I can't really remember ever losing a fight. Oh yeah, I guess there was that last time. But then, it only took one time. Well anyway, I wasn't unaccustomed to swapping punches, but there is nothing as ridiculous as a ghost and a near ghost trying to throw down. We went at it for a good ten minutes before deciding the effort was futile. We could make contact but the blows had little effect on either of us.

After our anger dissipated we separated. I said, "See, that was good effort. If you put that much emotion into contacting Caroline you'll be healed and back in her arms real fast."

"Yeah, you think so?"

"Absolutely."

"You better hope it works or I'll come back and kick your ass again."

"Well, in that case, I hope it works, too."

This time I waited while he tried. He grunted and strained – pressed palms to his head for added assistance, but nothing happened. After several long agonizing minutes, he stopped.

"Okay genius, what do you want me to try next?

What to do now? I paced. I was at a loss. It only made sense that there had to be a way back. My knowledge of how that might occur physiologically was limited, but logically the path had to exist.

The chances of finding a way inside Mac's head had been impossible at one time too. I'd figure this out. My attention was drawn to the thick gray mass surrounding us. I stopped a few feet short and studied the map-like fissures covering the surface. Did they serve a purpose or was it like soundproofing to prevent outside noise from penetrating Mac's consciousness and interrupting his healing sleep? We must be standing where his mind had been walled away for his protection.

"Maybe you have to push back these walls to get back to your body."

He looked from me to the walls and back to me, then made a face that said, "Right!"

"Hey, I'm serious. It makes sense. Besides, what else you got to do? You're just hanging out here.

Mac reached out and put a tentative finger on the wall. It pushed in like sponge. Rubbing his fingers together, he said, "It's wet."

"Yeah, would you want your brain to be dry?"

"Guess not." Placing his hand on the wall he pushed

harder. His hand sank in to the wrist. He pulled out and his hand made a sucking, slurp-like sound. The wall returned to its original shape. "I don't think that's going to work. It gives but comes back. There's no way to push it all back at once."

"You don't need to push it all back. You just need a path back. Just something you can squeeze through."

Mac stood facing the wall and placed both hands on the surface. He pushed. Again the sponge gave way. He attempted to step into it. He pushed harder, stepped in deeper, and the wall closed around him. He disappeared from view.

I waited. Then there was a violent commotion at the spot he went in. Muffled cries for help reached me. I stepped forward and tried to find a spot to reach in and grab for Mac. I was unable to make the wall move or even indent. I stepped back in panic. *Damn! Mac got swallowed up by his brain.*

CHAPTER

Eighteen

I popped into the hospital room. Caroline wasn't back yet, but I wasn't sure how much real time had passed. Concentrating with all my will, I was able to blink directly into Mac's head in time to see a foot emerge from the gooey wall. I dove, wrapped my hands around the appendage, and pulled.

Soon I had a leg free. After that an arm. When Mac broke into the clear he collapsed on the floor, breathing hard, and spitting little gray globules around the room. He had tiny, sticky gray matter pieces all over him.

After a while he sat up, still silent. I squatted next to him, waiting as patiently as I could for him to recover enough to speak. Instead, he frowned and punched me in the face. I didn't bother responding. I deserved it, if only for manipulating him.

Fifteen minutes later, I was back to my pacing. For some reason, I still felt the secret was in moving the wall. Mac just stood there, silent. His sigh interrupted my train of thought. "Maybe I'm not meant to go back, until I'm ready or …"

"Hey, hey, hey, wait a minute. Don't go giving up on me – in either direction. I can't quit now, not having come this far."

"You mean *I* can't quit."

"Huh?"

"You said *you* can't quit. Seems to me I'm the one doing all the work."

"Ah, yeah, I meant we as in us working together. You want to be alive and see your girlfriend; I want to save lives. Not trying to be a dick here, but you do the math. You want to save yourself; I'm trying to save thousands."

He looked at me, incredulous. "Seriously? You went there? As if my lack of success is me not caring to help. I agreed to go back so I *could* help. Yes, to see Caroline too, but I wouldn't have even tried this insanity if not for you. And for the record, you are a dick."

I had to admit, that was low, even for me. "Yeah, you're right. I'm sorry. I know you're trying and I do appreciate your efforts. I'm just feeling stressed because I know time's running out. Mac, I don't want the burden of responsibility for those lives to fall on me because I failed them. Can you understand that? That's an eternity in hell for me no matter if I end up there or not."

My words seemed to calm him for the moment. He leaned back against the wall. It gave, but supported him. "Okay. What's next?"

I smiled. "Thanks, Mac. I've been giving it some thought. Maybe you have to mentally peel away the layers. Picture a path through to being awake. In fact, maybe it's as easy as thinking yourself awake, like after a good night's sleep."

"Well, if that's the best you've …"

"It is for now. Process of elimination and all that stuff."

He moved to the center of the room and turned a slow circle. He took a few breaths and nodded.

"Okay, I'll be watching. Remember, 'bomb.'"

"Yeah. I have a feeling that'll be the easy part." I teleported back to the room and watched. It wasn't long before I saw Mac's eyes widened and he gasped. A quick whimper escaped his lips and everyone in the room jumped to their feet. I waited expectantly, but Mac said nothing else. His body shuddered for a moment then stilled. He looked like death and that scared me.

Alarms beeped. Panic seized Mac's family as wails of emotion filled the room.

Sandra ran from the room to get a nurse. Caroline and Barney were yelling for Garrett to come back to them. A cacophony exploded into the room. Medical personnel filled the tiny space. The family was ushered out and the staff went to work with frantic, practiced experience.

Cold fear crept through my essence. It didn't look good. I wasn't a medical expert, but I knew a flat line when I saw one. I had killed Garrett, or at least hastened his death.

In a second I was back inside Mac's head. He was lying death-like still on the floor. I moved toward his inert form but was yanked backwards off my feet. In a flash the wall had me wrapped up. It perceived me as a threat and for good reason. I couldn't see or move. As guilt enveloped me, I stopped struggling. At that point I was expelled from Mac's consciousness.

CHAPTER

Nineteen

I climbed to the sky. I couldn't miss his light now. It pulsed in a strong rhythm. Though Mac's life force hadn't launched heavenward yet, it was little comfort to me. Guilt consumed me like flesh-eating worms. Desperate to know Mac's fate, I was afraid my re-entry would be denied by his brain's protective system.

Hovering above his light beam, I replayed the events that occurred in Mac's hospital room. Though concerned, I couldn't contain my excitement by the fact that he had done it. Mac had broken free of his coma, if only for a fraction of a second. He was there. I heard him. We all had heard him. Convinced now more than ever that this could work, I had to find a way for him to go back and stay just a little longer. My heart raced as I considered the possibilities. I might yet be able to stop that bomb from exploding.

Buoyed by the possibility of success with my own goals to the forefront, I attempted to reenter Mac's mind. The beam was solid and strong, meaning that his life must still be in jeopardy. I transported back into his hospital room. The medical personnel were still actively working around Mac's body, but they'd been able to restart his heart. Though his pulse was weak he was still alive, at least for the time being.

Since I'd already established a path to his brain from here, I made the leap and was surprised to find I was able to gain entry. I turned in fast circles, waiting for the wall to encapsulate me as before, but nothing happened. Mac was writhing on the floor, arms wrapped around his head. He squeezed hard, as if the added pressure to his skull from the outside would balance that within. I dropped to my knees beside him and tried to figure a way to ease his pain.

"Mac! Mac, can you hear me? What can I do to help?"

Through gritted teeth he said, "Eat shit and die again."

I held his body to me and tried to draw his pain into me. Tears of frustration dripped from my face. Maybe not real tears, but they felt like they were. His pain was as real to me as if it was my own. In a sense I guess it was, since I was the one who'd convinced him to go back.

And yet, in the back of my mind I was already thinking about how to get Garrett to try again. It had worked. I saw his lips move. I heard the gasp and the whimper and so did everyone in that room. I had found a way to make contact. A bolt of exhilaration rushed through me.

Was it fair to put Mac through that kind of anguish again for my own gains? The answer was easy for me: *Hell yeah, it was!* But then again, I didn't have to feel the pain either. Not proud of my decision but knowing I wouldn't change my mind, I mumbled a worthless prayer of forgiveness. I lifted Mac's head and put it in my lap to comfort him, and began plotting my next strategy.

This had to be handled with great care. If I pushed too hard, the pain might kill Garrett before he could deliver the message. Then I'd be forced to start all over. With time running down, who knew if I'd ever find another portal to the real world in time? Well, perhaps one entity did. I looked up. Did I even dare ask His help? No, that would definitely cross a line. Right; like I hadn't already crossed every one I'd ever drawn for myself.

I wasn't proud of what I'd done or was about to do. All I

could hope for now was that somewhere, understanding of the situation was being recorded for my eventual court martial and non-stop flight to the nether regions.

I looked down at Mac and saw that he was no longer trembling. He appeared calm. His eyelids fluttered then flew open. Green eyes blazed a hatred that pierced what was left of my soul. I understood this raw emotion but would have to find a way to deal with Mac's ire somehow.

"I'm sorry, Mac. I truly didn't know." Within a beat, my empathy changed to excitement. "But it worked ... you broke through! Your mother and father and Caroline heard you! You gave them new hope. Rest up and we'll try again."

The spark in his eyes ignited. He tried to speak but only spittle, grunts, and foam came out.

I patted his shoulder. "Good. I'm glad to hear you want to try again. I'll be back later to help you." Gently, I placed Mac's head on the floor and stood. "Get some rest now." I smiled, feeling like a winning coach during a post-game pep talk, and said, "And man, what a great effort."

Before he could respond I blinked out of there. It wasn't until I had reached my home cloud that I thought, *"What if he doesn't let me back in?"*

CHAPTER

Twenty

I called out to Les. It was the first time he didn't show up in a flash. He made me wait. He was either busy guiding someone else or I had pissed him off with my actions and behaviors and he was punishing me. I guess I deserved that, but it wasn't like I was doing it for myself. Who did it really hurt? Okay, maybe Garrett a little, but he'd get over it. This time.

Besides, it wasn't my fault. If they'd have just let me go back for one day, I could take care of this.

In the distance from above, Les' disembodied voice boomed around me like a clap of thunder. "Dream on."

I sighed. I was in for a long wait but I needed answers and Les was the only one who could give them to me.

I conjured up a kegerator, surprised when the cooler appeared before my eyes. However, my elation was short lived when I discovered it was empty. No amount of my effort would put a keg inside. The old polka song about drinking beer on Earth because there was none in heaven began playing in my head. I kicked the kegerator. "Now I know this is hell."

While Les kept me waiting, I ran through a myriad of possible scenarios and solutions to help manage Mac's pain. Clearly his body hadn't healed enough to allow his consciousness through without severe pain. I had to find a way to control his pain or he'd never be able to deliver the message. Man, no wonder I'd spent most of my years fighting for others. I was all heart.

I was well aware of time passing—time that had become a countdown to the end of so many lives. The thought of standing by, not being able to help them was almost more than I could bear. I paced my little cloud cubicle, the pressure building within me until I thought I might explode. Fighting back urge after urge to go back to Mac, I moved my lawn chair in front of the squad picture and sat down.

After once again reliving the nightmare that had claimed so many of them, I launched into a monologue, explaining the situation to them as I'd done countless times before. Alive or dead, I'd always felt they'd had my back. Although if I ever saw them again, I would have to ask where they were when I got killed. Most likely they were all hungover.

It dawned on me then that I'd never really been that close to anyone since then. I'd walled off that part of my emotions, not allowing anyone else near for fear of losing them too. That last picture of that ragged bunch of hard-nosed fighting men hanging on my cloud wall was all I had to brainstorm to. I know they'd understand, but what would *they* do?

Of course, I received no response. I needed to go somewhere I could think. An image flashed and something changed. Looking down, I saw grass. Scanning my new surroundings, I found I was now on a familiar baseball diamond, specifically a high school field. A flood of memories washed over me. Whenever I had a bad game I walked outfield grass from foul line to foul line, using the field as my sounding board. Even after I graduated high school I returned to that diamond to mull over important decisions in my life.

It was on this field that I decided to enlist in the army.

This field also saw my return as a Ranger. I would stand on the pitcher's mound and stare at home plate. My dead comrades would be in the field in defensive positions and the enemy would come up to bat and be mowed down by my team. Sometimes I saw the faces of the men I'd killed face to face. I offered no apologies; they uttered no curses. It was what it was. It was over. And now I was like them.

The last time I was on this field was more than six years ago after learning my neighbor's fourteen year old daughter had been kidnapped and gang raped. She was never the same after her ordeal. She would be haunted by her memory just as I was haunted by my own.

That was the first time I took the law into my own hands to help a victim and it was the most satisfying mission of my life. I found the punks who violated her; that part was easy. They were members of a local street gang. When I found the first one, he told me through his tears that they took Nicole because she had turned down a member who asked her out on a date. They thought Nicole acted like she was too good for them so they taught her a lesson.

The sad truth was that Nicole wanted to go out with the guy but her mother and father felt she was still too young to date. When I told that to the scumbag who'd asked her out, he cried and said he was sorry just before I smashed his face beyond any hope of recognition.

In my anger and need to avenge Nicole I put eleven gang members in the hospital and one didn't make it. Most would never be the same. To me that was justice and justice became my new calling. I'm sure there's a thread marking that decision.

CHAPTER

Twenty-One

Stopping on the pitcher's mound, I glanced up and asked, "Les, what would you do? Come on, man. You were alive once. You must have cared for someone. If the people you loved were in danger, what would you do? Would you give up without trying? I can't. I'm not made that way. I have to keep going. Damn it, talk to me! I need your help."

When I got no response I got very angry. The next thing I knew, I was at the plate with a faceless pitcher throwing batting practice to me. Ball after ball in an endless steady rhythm, the pitches came in and I smashed them as hard as I could, willing them beyond the fence, over the school, and out of sight. Then I pounded the bat on the ground until it broke in half.

"Feeling better now?" Les glowered at me with arms folded across his chest.

"If you didn't come here to help then just leave. I don't need any of your bullshit at the moment."

"Nice attitude for someone who was begging for my help just a short while ago."

We stepped closer to each other and exchanged glares. It was the first time I had seen Les mad. If he filed reports to the Big Guy about my behavior, I could be on the southbound train in seconds, but I didn't care. I wouldn't want to stay in an uncaring world anyway, real or otherwise.

"I am not uncaring."

His comment made me wonder again if he could read my

mind.

"I'm just more realistic than you are. I've been here for a long time and know how things work."

"How about the words, 'With God all things are possible'?"

"Oh, don't start quoting religious phrases to me. I'll bury you in them."

"With or without you I'm going to try to make this possible."

"You can't alter the impossible."

"And how do I know it's impossible until I try?"

"Because I'm telling you it can't be done," Les shouted.

The change in his tone and the pain on his face sparked a realization in my mind—one that jumped straight to the tip of my tongue and leaped for freedom.

"Oh my God, you've tried haven't you?" I got very excited.

He stared at me but something had clicked in his eyes. I could see it. "Tell me. Did you try to find a way back?"

His tormented voice whispered, "Yes." Tears filled his eyes and he lost focus as his memories transported him to another place and time. He turned away.

My anger bled away. I was left with an aching heart for Les and whatever loss he had endured. But in that ache grew hope. With a one-track mind, I pushed aside feelings and pressed on. "Tell me about it, Les."

His silence dragged on and I let him be.

"I killed my wife."

Whoa! That wasn't what I was expecting. My wide eyes took him in. He read my shock.

"Not physically, but I was responsible, so it was no different than if I had put a gun to her head and pulled the trigger."

I thought about his statement and then made one of my own. "That's not true or you wouldn't be here now."

Les paused again, working his hands in a circle.

"And suddenly you're the expert here?" His eyes flashed but the glare faded in an instant. "I should have been there for my wife but I wasn't. I was drunk. Trying to drive home, I flipped the car and... well, here I am. My wife was pregnant. She wasn't due for another month. I got talked into going for one with the guys I worked with, and we all know there's no such thing as just one. I didn't think there'd be a problem. After all, the baby wasn't due yet.

"I should've called, but I really did think I was going for just one. Janae tried to call me when her contractions started but my phone was in the car. While I was inside the bar having a good time, snow began to fall. After an hour of waiting for me with her contractions coming more regularly and stronger, she gave up and decided to drive herself.

"Just about the time she left the house, I managed to pull away from my co-workers and was on my way home. I really wasn't much of a drinker and it didn't take me long to realize I was too drunk to drive. I picked up my phone to call Janae and saw I had a bunch of missed calls. I remember feeling a cold chill run up my spine. I tried to call her, but drunk as I was, I drove off the road and toppled down the side of a mountain.

"Not twenty minutes later, Janae had a severe contraction and her water broke. The combination of those things together caused her to slide through an intersection on the slippery road. She was broadsided by a pickup truck. Of course by then, I was already here.

"If I would have been there we'd both be alive. She didn't die at the scene. She continued to fight for life; if not hers, then for our unborn child's. Much like your Garrett, she lingered in between. I tried to find a way to get back to her, but there was nothing I could do. My pleas, like yours, fell on deaf ears."

Then Les' face went gray. His eyes glazed over.

"I watched her from up here, from the time the paramedics arrived to when they took her into surgery. I saw her resting in a coma with the same flickering life force that you saw. I didn't know what to do to help her. She lasted eighteen hours and then she died. They saved our baby girl. She lived for an hour before joining her mother. I died again with every passing minute." Les' voice cracked. "My poor judgment killed them both."

I didn't know how to respond, so for once I said nothing for quite a while. Then I asked. "Have you seen them here? Surely they're up here with you."

"No, I watched as her soul left her body and ascended. She shot right past me and straight to her final destination. Unlike her husband, she was a good person. She's where she belongs, and well, as you see, I'm where I belong."

"So she's up there waiting for you?"

"Well, she's up there, but I doubt she's waiting for me. By now she knows what a fool I am. What a loser I'd become. She knows I chose to have another beer rather than come home and that ultimately I was responsible for her death."

"I'm sure she has forgiven you and will want to be with you. You have an eternity to make things right by her. You've punished yourself enough."

Les' voice became hard. "And what do you credit that insight to? Have you seen her? Talked to her? You don't have a clue as to what she is feeling. And in case you haven't been paying attention, this is where our final judgment takes place. All the while we are here we are pleading our case without even realizing it. So even if I am punishing myself, there is still a greater power waiting to serve up my penalty. "

"That part I understand. There's nothing you can do about that. But surely, however long you've been here, you've been working to see them. And how do *you* know she hasn't forgiven you?"

Les turned his hard eyes at me. I met his gaze, but not to challenge him. "You can't live eternity in fear. Sooner or later you'll have to find out."

"Yes, sooner or later." He seemed to melt and become smaller. "Only the sooner is closer than the later."

I understood then. Les was afraid to move on. Was his fear what kept him here? Maybe he had to forgive himself before he could see his wife. "What do you mean?"

"I mean I may no longer have a choice in the matter. It is close to my time to move. I have almost fulfilled my obligations."

My brows knitted together in confusion.

"I don't understand. You have to prove your worthiness?"

"Something like that."

"Well if you've come this far, you must want to move on. What's left for you to do?"

He looked at me strangely and I was confused again.

"You."

"Me what?"

"*You* are what's left for me to do."

The light bulb flicked on. "Oh, Man!"

CHAPTER

Twenty-Two

Knowing the answer, I asked the question anyway. "What do I have to do with your moving on?"

"You are my last assignment. I must successfully integrate you into this world or prepare you for your journey to the next. You see my dilemma? As much as I may want to help you get back to earth, to do so would be seen as a failure. That would ruin my chance at moving up. I would be forced to start again.

"However, if I don't help you go back and eventually you become adjusted to your new surroundings, I will be allowed to ascend to where I will see my wife, if in fact she chooses to see me. Your success frightens me the most, because as much as I want to be reunited with Janae, I *am* afraid to face her. I could accept God's judgment even if it meant an eternity here for my crime. But Janae's," he shook his head. "No, that I can't do. God may change his mind but Janae never will. Once she has judged, that verdict will stand, overturning God's decision and eternity."

"If you fail, how much longer will you be forced to stay?"

"I don't know. I guess I'll find out if I fail with you."

"Nothing like added pressure on a guy. That is a dilemma. I don't know what to say. It doesn't sound like you're ready to see your wife yet."

He turned his eyes toward me. "What's that supposed to mean?"

"I don't know. I guess I was trying to justify what I have in mind. Look, I don't mean to upset you or get you in trouble. I wish I could just sit by and let those people die. But if I did nothing and those souls came up here, how could I face *them?* Some of them are bound to end up here. They will know I did nothing to prevent their deaths. It's the same fear you have."

I stood and began animated pacing. My arms flailed about as I talked.

"Well, except I wasn't married to any of them or got any of them pregnant—that I know of. But look at it this way: you've been given a second chance to help save someone. Will you be able to face them, knowing you could've made a difference?"

"I will not see them."

"Huh?"

"I will not see them. You can only see those beings that you somehow had contact with on earth."

I was speechless—but not for too long.

"Seriously?"

"Yes seriously. That's how it works. You can follow the life of anyone you've had contact with in some way. Your circles here can expand based on other souls you meet who have had some connection to those souls you knew. That's how you can get into a baseball game. You have to know someone who knows someone and be invited into their circle."

"No, I meant seriously, that's your response? '*You won't see them?'* Is that how you justify it? You won't worry about their deaths because you won't have to see them afterwards? How do you live with yourself?"

"Listen you, just because you came here doesn't mean

you're going to stay. I can fail you, too, you know. If you fail here you are out of options, if you know what I mean. So don't be giving me any attitude. That's definitely no way to get on my good side, especially if you're trying to ask for my help. And truly, with the pain you are causing that man, who are you play on my guilt? You should be ashamed of what you are doing that poor soul."

A spark of hope lit my eyes. I pushed everything else Les said aside and focused on the one thing. "Help? You'll help me? Please, Les. Let's try together. I'm sorry if I offended you. It's just that time is running out."

"I haven't decided yet. I'm not really sure what I can do to help you. Besides, you don't seem to understand what that might mean. If you break the rules you could be sent packing in an instant—and I don't think you'd like the journey south."

Closing my eyes, I tried to picture eternal damnation. Whether it was in hell or a brand of hell of my own making, one was the same as the other. "Yeah, even if that's the end result I'll exist with it."

"Oh yeah, tough guy? What about abolishment of soul?"

CHAPTER Twenty-Three

"Huh? Abominal? What?"

"The absolute finality is for the soul of the offending to be abolished. To be no more for eternity, never to be returned anywhere, at any time, for any purpose. You cease. Period.

"Actually, that sounds better than eternal damnation."

"You may avoid the pain, but if your soul still exists, you are still alive in one sense. Your memories stay intact. You can still be at peace."

"Les, from what you know about me so far, do you really think that would be a concern to me? If the only memories I had left were full of my failure, why have any?"

He nodded, understanding. "Still, I thought you should be aware of the consequences. There is a lot to lose, especially if that boy dies because of your involvement."

I thought about that for a moment. This was so unfair. If the Powers That Be knew anything about my life then surely they had to understand that I had to make the effort. How could they punish me for wanting to save lives?

"So let me get this straight. If I disobey the Almighty I could spend eternity in hell or be abolished, even though my intent is to save a bunch of lives. Is that what you're telling me?"

"Obviously, if you do something against His wishes you will be banished. I can't say for certain what will happen if you manage to somehow contact earth, but are you willing to take that chance?"

"Well, maybe the better question is, do I want to stay in a place that tries to discourage a newly dead person from wanting to save the lives of others? I guess the answer to your question is yes. I would be willing to sacrifice my eternal soul for the chance to save those people."

"But you don't even know them. How can it matter to you?"

I looked him in the eyes. I wondered if he was testing me. After a moment I decided it didn't matter. My mind was made up. "If you have to ask me that, then you don't know me and I'm not sure I want to know you."

"And how far do you think you'd get here without my help?"

"Seems to me I'm already working without your help."

A spark of anger lit his eyes. "Now that's unfair. If you want my help in any matter that I am allowed to help with I'll do everything I can, but this—this is just crazy. You are asking me to risk too much. You might not care about where you end up, but I do."

"So you do want to see your wife, then? Or do you think you can avoid her for eternity?"

"You are twisting things around. This is about you, not me."

"That's not what you just said. I would've thought that if you'd tried as hard as you say you did to get to her when she was dying then you would try just as hard to get to her now. Did love die? Did you lose hope? Faith?"

"That's different. I already explained the situation to you."

"Did you really try to see her or were you afraid then too?"

He turned on me and appeared bigger, suddenly imposing. The heat of his intensity scorched me as if I was standing too close to a fire. I thought he was about to explode on me. Although I couldn't touch him, I wasn't so sure he couldn't do some damage to me. Still, I decided if he took a swing at me, I wouldn't defend myself. For my own purposes I had pushed him kind of hard. If he hit me, I deserved it.

Bracing myself for the onslaught, I locked eyes with him and waited. Instead of pummeling me, Les opted for a quick exit. Before I could apologize he was gone.

CHAPTER

Twenty-Four

I waited as long as I could, then moved to my cloud and paced in ever widening circles. Patience was not one of my strong suits. Time was still running out. I needed Les' help. Even if he wasn't willing to get involved, I still needed his knowledge. But one way or another, I *was* going to continue.

"Les! Come back!" I shouted. "I'm sorry. Please come back. I just want to ask you some questions. I promise nothing personal. I want to understand how things work here and then I won't bother you anymore."

I looked up. Nothing. I continued walking in circles, my neck twisting left and right to detect any movement. When he didn't show, I walked to the floating picture and stared at it. I let some of the better memories flash before my eyes. "I wish you guys were here. I know you'd help me."

"I'm not heartless, you know."

The voice startled me. I jumped, icy fingers running up my spine. Imagine that—a ghost being spooked.

"It's not that I don't want to help you, I'm just bound by a different set of rules that you seem unwilling to accept."

"And you always play by the rules?"

"I can't help being me anymore than you can help being you."

Okay, that made sense. At least he was speaking to me again. "Well then, let me ask you something. Back on earth, there were always stories about people seeing ghosts. There were reports of communication with the dead and crossing over to the other side. Was any of that true?"

Les frowned. "Yes and no, but you're not going to like the answer."

"Lay it on me."

"The ghosts you hear about mostly do not exist. The ones that do are stuck on earth most likely for eternity. Their souls, the lights you saw, for whatever reason never left earth. They chose to stay there instead of taking a chance on where they might end up otherwise.

"Most spirits down there are evil. Some just stayed because they were in love with someone still alive. Their feelings were so strong that love's pull was more powerful than death's. Each soul has its own reason for being there. For you, maybe the reason was you weren't evil enough to want to stay, or you didn't have a love so powerful that it captured your soul."

"So there's no chance for me of being conjured or contacted through a séance or median?"

"No, and that's *medium*."

I paused long enough to load my next batch of questions.

"Okay, let me ask you this. Why didn't it work when you tried to enter your wife's life force?"

Les got a faraway look. "I'm not really sure. Perhaps because I was brand new here, like you are now, and didn't have a clue how things worked. Even though I saw her light, I didn't know what it meant. I had no idea about how to help Janae, or enter her life force. I learned what the light was later from my transition counselor, but if he knew the secret to get inside he never told me what it was.

"If I'd had that information, I still might not have been able to save her, but I could have been there for her at the end to comfort her. I could have told her I was sorry and that

I loved her. And who knows; maybe being there then might have made a difference. I'll never know." He paused. His sorrow evident on his face and in his eyes. "Anyway, you got a lot farther than I did."

"But the point is you wanted to try. How did you feel when there was no one there to guide you? If only your transition counselor had given you some advice or even some encouragement, maybe it would've changed the outcome. At the very least, Janae would know you tried to save her."

"Yeah. I guess that's true. But it's too late now. So why think about the 'what ifs'?"

Getting angry, I shouted. "Stop saying that. You tried, damn it! You wanted to be there for her. It wasn't your fault you didn't know how. You can't keep beating yourself up over something you had no control over."

Les yelled back. "I had control over stopping for a stupid drink. I could've just said no."

"Did you ever stop to think that maybe it all would've happened anyway? Isn't 'it was meant to be' one of the biggest clichés among the living? Sorry to bring it up, but maybe there was nothing you could've done anyway. If it was your time or hers, you couldn't alter that."

Les shook his head, the anger draining away. "What difference does it make now? No matter what, there is no way to change what happened. Wishing doesn't make it so."

"But Les, there is still time to change a future outcome for me. It's not in the past. It's not too late. This bomb is going off in a little more than two days days."

"I don't know that there is anything I can tell you that will help. But using your same logic, what if the loss of those lives was meant to be?"

I paused. In truth, I had thought about that. With a sigh, I said, “Then so be it, but it won't be because I didn't try.”

“Just so you understand that no matter what, if those people are supposed to die, nothing you do can prevent their deaths.”

He had a great point, but I'd come so far already, I couldn't stop now.

“It’s like on the baseball diamond.” I envisioned the field and we were there. “Our motto was always ‘If we go down, let’s make sure we go down swinging, not talking’. I can face those people if they die, knowing in my heart I did everything possible to save them.”

We were standing on the pitcher’s mound. I was in my old uniform. The glove on my hand felt good; the smell of leather igniting grand memories. For that one instant I was a star again, taking the mound to get the team out of a jam.

Les looked around and nodded. “You’re learning, grasshopper.”

I lifted my hand toward Les and opened the glove wide. He looked at me quizzically. “Give me the ball, Coach. Let me try to win this game,” I said.

Les looked down, surprised to see the baseball in his hand. “I don’t suppose you’ve created a hot dog vendor?” He slapped the ball into my mitt. “Save the game, Swifty.”

CHAPTER

Twenty-Five

"Okay, I will try to guide you, but there's one thing we have yet to discuss and it will determine how far I will help you."

"What's that?"

The baseball diamond was gone and we were back on my cloud, staring down at the faint lifeline of Garrett MacIntosh.

"Him." He nodded toward Mac.

"There is still a chance he may pull through. We have no way of seeing his future. If what you are about to do kills him when he was going to live, you will alter the world and the lives of all which he would have had contact with during his life. That may ultimately affect more people than you are trying to save. Can you understand that?"

My eyes widened. "Wow! I hadn't thought about that."

"And that's why a smarter head is now guiding you. The pain he felt when you sent him back the first time was real. I'm sure the doctors have him medicated, but since he cannot speak to them, they can only guess at his pain level.

"What he felt before was beyond his pain threshold. The only way for this to succeed is for him to reconnect in slow stages. Do not try to send him all the way back. It will be too much and his heart may not be able to handle the shock."

Les continued his counseling and for the first time since I'd been there, I appreciated it. "Instead, only send his consciousness back to attempt contact. Do it in short bursts."

"Yeah, that's good thinking."

"Of course, we haven't taken into consideration one very important thing. He may not want to go back."

"I guess it will be up to me to convince him."

"Remember, you cannot force him. Mac has to want to go back."

"I'll do my best."

"Chance, you need to listen. It is very important that Mac makes the decision to go back on his own. You can give him reasons why he would want to go back, but you cannot trick or force him to go back. If he dies because of you, it will be no different than if you murdered him. Do you understand what I'm telling you?"

"Yeah Les, I understand," I said with a hint of attitude. "I don't want to hurt Mac. I need his help, but I still respect his free will."

That seemed to satisfy him.

"Notice the lower portion of the light is faded and thinning. It is no longer blinking. His tie to the world is becoming weaker. If the light loses contact with the world, it means he has died. His soul will be free and there will be nothing you can do. You will have to work fast. Just a suggestion: try to enter at the weakest point, obviously trying not to sever the connection with his body."

"Okay, Coach. And Les, thanks. I appreciate the risk you're taking."

"I hope so. A lot of lives and souls depend on you. Good luck." He offered his hand and I took it. For the briefest of moments I felt pressure against my hand. The hint of a smile tugged at the corner of his lips.

With that, I dove off my cloud, replaying Les' words about Mac in my head. He had to say it, but I felt guilty. I was in a no-win situation. To save a bunch I might end up sacrificing a few. I felt like I was in a Star Trek movie. But in this case, if I screwed up, everyone would lose. I accelerated toward the small cone of light that was Garrett, hoping he would listen to reason. Of course, I was talking about my reason, not his.

Without stopping, I hit the narrowest possible connection to earth and bore through. Mac was lying on a beach he had constructed from some memory. The sun he'd conjured was warm enough to leave a glisten of perspiration on his face. His eyes were closed and he was humming some melody that was so far out of tune it was impossible to recognize.

I made a slow descent and landed in front of him. My body became a shield blocking the sun from his face. He opened his eyes.

"Oh, no way. You have to go. I don't want to talk to you."

"Mac, please listen. You're my only hope. You are the only person capable of saving thousands of innocent people. Didn't you ever want to be a hero?"

"No! Now leave me alone." He closed his eyes again. "And get out of my sun."

"I don't believe it. You're going to let all those people die? What do you think will happen when you get to heaven and all those who died know it was because you were getting a tan and couldn't be bothered to help? They're going to hate you. You'll never get your wings … just because you were selfish."

"Wings?" He sat up. "You actually get—wait, I'm not listening." Mac covered his ears and resumed humming.

I raised my voice. "Oh, but wait; what am I saying? If you let all those people die you're not gonna make it to heaven anyway. You'll still be a hero though, only it will be in hell. Hell, they'll probably erect a damn statue to you! You'll be listed with all the other mass murderers in history."

Wait. Wasn't this lying and trickery? I realized I was shouting, rambling, and just making shit up, but I couldn't stop myself. I was angry and desperate. "You'll sit at the right hand of the devil in the hottest seat of honor. Won't that make your fiancée happy? Only she'll never get to see you because you know she'll be in heaven. It won't take long for all those people to tell her what you did—or didn't do, I should say—and where you are."

"Stop it!" Mac screamed, looking like he was about to explode. I started getting nervous about his condition and jumped into the hospital room again. His heart rate had increased dramatically. His father ran to get a nurse. The room erupted with frantic, yet controlled activity from the staff and building fearful emotion from the family. Concern showed on everyone's faces, including mine.

I sighed and popped back into Mac's brain.

Mac was speed pacing in a small circle holding his head with both hands, and shouting, "No!" over and over.

I sat in the sand and stared out at the endless beach. If he was so damned creative, why didn't he put in a lake?

I didn't know what to do. I desperately wanted to talk to Mac, but didn't want to be responsible for deepening his coma either. I waited. After Mac had calmed down and finished his pacing, he stopped in front of me and dropped his hands to his sides.

"Why are you crying? Aren't you dead already?"

Brushing my eyes, my hand came away wet. I was unaware the tears had been falling. I looked at him. "I'm sorry. I swear I'm not here to hurt you."

"Good, 'cause I'm not going to let you hurt me again." Then he kicked sand in my face.

CHAPTER

Twenty-Six

"I'm sorry about the last time," I said. "I didn't know that would happen."

"Why don't you just go away and leave me alone?"

I stood, brushing the sand from my clothes. "Can I make a deal with you?"

"No."

The beach disappeared and we were back to the nothingness of his mind. I mean, oh, never mind.

The anger flared but I swallowed it. "Just let me explain, and afterwards if you still say no, I won't bother you again. I promise."

"I don't need to listen to you at all."

I let out a long, slow, defeated breath. "No you don't, but I'm asking you as a fellow soul to give me a chance. Believe me, it's not for me."

"I know it's probably to save a loved one of yours, right?"

"No; actually, I don't know any of the victims. I was trying to stop some terrorists from setting off a bomb. I failed, and because of that those people will die. You understand? I made a stupid mistake and it cost me my life. As if that wasn't bad enough I'm now responsible for all those other lives."

"Oh, bullshit! How can you be responsible for their lives when you're dead? You can't blame yourself for that. I think you're just using me. You figured out how to live again and need me to help you."

"No!" I shouted. My fists clenched so tight the bones felt like they might snap. "Mac, I swear, this has nothing to do with me going back. I can't go back. I can't take over your body or anything like that. All I'm trying to do is get a message through to someone who can defuse the bomb."

I clapped my hands to my face and dragged them downward. "If I just would've gone to the police I could've stopped the terrorists before they got started, but I didn't. Please Mac. Give me one more chance. There is no way I can go back. All I'm asking is for you to deliver a warning."

Mac said nothing, but I could see he was thinking. I pressed ahead. "Look, what if I told you I think I have a way for you to communicate with your family and perhaps do it with a lot less pain? I've been giving this a lot of thought. It doesn't do either of us any good for you to be hurt."

I stared expectantly. He mirrored me but his face held no discernible expression. As the silence stretched on I hoped it meant that Mac was giving my pleas serious consideration.

At last he spoke. "Will I be able to see them?"

My heart leapt. "No. Opening your eyes might cause you too much pain. This will happen so fast you won't be able to hear them either. This is as new to me as it is to you. If you go back, we'll both learn what to do next. Perhaps if my idea works, communication can be two ways. I just don't know for sure."

"Will I be a ghost? Do I have to die to make this work?"

"No. In fact, I'm hoping I can figure out how to bring you out of this coma. I want to send you back alive."

"Really? You can do that?"

The excitement in his voice was too much to ask for. It would've been so easy to lie to him, but I couldn't do it. "I can't make that promise. I'm not gonna lie to you. It's all in theory. I'm not God. I'm just some guy who can't turn his back on a world he's no longer a part of. I can't give you a guarantee. None of it may work. What if I can't send you back? What if in the end you die anyway? Wouldn't it still be worth the effort to at least have been able to say goodbye to your loved ones?"

"You're just using me. You don't care if I live or die."

I had to work through my frustration to form my next sentences. "I do care if you live and yes, I am using you. I'm not denying that. But it has nothing to do with me. I won't get anything out of this—except peace, I hope."

I slid a hand through my hair and walked away. An image of Monica's face flashed in my mind's eye.

"Maybe that's not entirely true." I turned and faced Mac. "I found out that three days after I was killed I would have met my wife. If I wouldn't have stuck my nose in someone else's business I wouldn't be here. I would have found the peace and happiness I never thought would be mine again. It would've been a good life, I think. Of course, I'll never really know." I closed my eyes and swallowed hard. Taking a few breaths I opened my eyes and continued.

"I lost a lot when I died. Who doesn't, I suppose." I shrugged. "If I'd lived I would've had a future, but then the people who have the bomb would kill thousands anyway. Who knows; I could have been one of them. Maybe I was just destined to die at that time one way or another.

"So I guess I do have an interest in this. I want to stop the bombers. That's the truth, but doing so will not only save those lives, but I'll get my revenge on my killers. It will be payback for them stealing my future. So yeah, I'm using you. You're my only hope—my only possible contact with anyone still alive. To say I'm desperate would be an understatement. I wish I could go back in your place, but it just doesn't work that way. I'm sorry to say, but you're all I've got. Knowing the risks to you, it's hard to ask, but I have to. Will you at least try?"

He stopped pacing and was no longer yelling for me to leave. That gave me hope. What else did I have?

CHAPTER Twenty-Seven

"I want to help, but I'm afraid. That last time I felt the most excruciating pain I'd ever felt. If I was in that much pain when I had my accident, no wonder my mind hid me away here. I just want to stay here and rest until the pain is gone. Then I won't be afraid to wake up."

I sighed, knowing I was losing him. "I understand, but consider this: what if you don't wake up? What if you die or worse, stay in a coma until your family decides to pull the plug? If this works they'll at least know you're still in here. It will delay their decision to unplug you, no matter what the doctors say. But if the end does come, you may have a chance to say goodbye, right?"

We looked at each other, neither knowing what else to say. We'd given our pitches. It was Mac's choice and nothing I said could make him do what he didn't want to do.

My eyes fell first. Defeat was imminent. My head sagged and my shoulders slumped. "Okay, I'm sorry I hurt you. Good luck. I hope you get well soon."

Throwing my hands into the air, I was about to do my Superman imitation and leap skyward toward my cloud, even though apparently, all I had to do was think about my new home and I would be there, when I heard, "Wait."

I almost fell trying to stop. There was still a lot I had to learn about getting around.

Righting myself, I faced him with hopeful expectation.

"What-what was your plan to control the pain?"

I smiled. "Thank you for at least listening. I hope it works, but I'm gonna be honest with you. There still may be some pain. My plan is to try and control it from both sides. When you open your protective wall only do just enough to squeeze through. Leave the majority in place to limit your exposure. This next part will sound stupid, but to control the pain on the other side, you will have to go back and actually say something like, 'I need more drugs.' Then pop back out again before the pain gets too bad. I'll watch from your room. If they understand and up your dosage, the next time the pain should be bearable enough for you to pass the message along."

Mac's mouth had dropped open. That wasn't a good sign.

In haste, I tried to recover. "I know it's risky, but you know what to expect this time. In and out. Say the words and get out. You can do this."

"It's gonna hurt," He winced

"Yes, but only for a few seconds. Can you do it?"

"Man, if this kills me I'm going to haunt you forever."

"Mac, if this kills you I probably won't be anywhere you can reach me. But rest assured I'll be feeling more pain than you and on a daily basis."

He frowned and then seemed to understand. "So you're willing to face eternal damnation to try to save people you have never met?

"Yes, and I'm willing to stake your life on it."

"Great."

"It was just a joke."

"Yeah; I'm laughing to death here."

"Sorry. But the other bad thing …"

"You mean other than the pain or my possible death?"

"Yeah. The other bad thing is that even after all this effort it may not work or your family might not understand what you are saying."

"That would be bad, yeah."

"Just wanted to be honest. After all, you're the one taking all the risk."

"Glad you noticed that. Yet you still want to sacrifice my life for this salvation plan?"

"You're the only one who can decide if the risk is worth the reward. I wish I could do it. I really do. I'd do it in a heartbeat, but that's me. Are you still willing to try?"

Mac looked away. He rubbed a hand over his face a few times. "What's it like? You know, up there."

"To tell you the truth, I don't know. I'm so recently dead I haven't had time to explore much. Plus I've kinda been obsessed with this bomb thing. I'm sure it's nice if you take the time to look around and make contact with loved ones and friends."

"You haven't seen anyone from your family yet?"

"No, and I'm kinda short in the friend department."

"Gee, there's a surprise."

"Yeah, thanks. Besides, I'm not sure many of my friends would've made it this far north—if you know what I mean. Actually, I'm surprised I made it this far. But who knows how long that will last after this."

"So my success is tied to yours?"

"Let's just say we both have a lot riding on this."

Silence descended over us. There was nothing left to discuss. He was either going to do it or not. Finally, he threw his arms up and shrugged.

"All right, let's do this. Just remember what I said about the eternal haunting."

I smiled, but was thinking that would be the least of my

worries.

CHAPTER

Twenty-Eight

As I left, Mac was doing some deep breathing, trying to prepare himself for the journey back into his body. I was nervous about leaving him for fear he'd change his mind without my support…well, my constant nagging and guilt-pressured mind games, but in the end it was always his decision.

The room had changed since I was last there. The momentary hope had faded into quiet depression. Barney was out walking the halls, a nurse was changing a drip bag, and both Sandra and Caroline had their heads down, staring at the floor. Their faces and bodies sagged from exhaustion. Neither woman looked like they could take much more stress. I hoped this would work if only for their sakes; to give them renewed hope that Mac was still in there somewhere, fighting for his life, while the many injuries slowly healed.

In my current state it was difficult to determine how much time had passed. It felt like a long time since I left Mac. Even though the clock had barely moved, I began to panic. I was about to jump back to see what Mac was doing when his entire body convulsed.

The sudden movement startled the nurse and she missed the hook. The bag dropped to the floor. The monitor beeped as Mac's heart rate soared. The nurse fumbled with buttons on machines while staring at the monitor readings.

The two women were on their feet in a second. They

rushed to the bed. Caroline sobbed and the mother let out shrill, pained squeaks.

Mac groaned loud enough to be heard down the hall. The sound of approaching footsteps echoed louder as they neared the door.

In a voice so pained and deep it sounded as if Satan had possessed his body, Mac said, "…gs. More drugs," and his body went slack. It happened so fast no one had time to react. Mac's body went so limp that I was afraid he was actually dead this time. I wanted to run to him to help him through the trauma but I needed to see if anyone in the room understood what he said.

"Did you hear that?" His mother was the first to speak.

The nurse was taking Mac's pulse and wasn't listening. Her hands shook visibly.

"Oh my God, he spoke!" exclaimed Caroline. She turned to the nurse. "Does that mean he's coming out of it? Is he going to live?"

Another nurse preceded Mac's father into the room. A doctor followed seconds later.

"He asked for more drugs. You heard it," Mac's mother said to the nurse. She turned to the doctor as he approached the bed. "My son's in pain. He needs more medication."

The doctor and the first nurse ignored her while they rechecked Mac's vitals. Numbers and lines jumped and peaks and valleys still filled the screen, but so far no flat line.

"Tell him," she commanded the nurse. "You heard it too, Caroline. You heard what Garrett said! Tell the doctor."

"It's true," Caroline said through her sobs. "He woke up and spoke to us. He said, 'Drugs, more drugs.' We all heard him."

The doctor looked at the nurse for confirmation. Though still shaking, she managed to reattach the IV bag and nod. "That's what he said."

The doctor reached through the bandages and lifted Garrett's eyelid and flashed a penlight into the pupil. "Did he open his eyes and look around or just speak?"

The nurse responded, "He just spoke. He startled me half to death." She blushed and glanced at Mac's mother. "Ah, sorry." To the doctor she added, "I didn't see him open his eyes."

He turned toward the family.

"Just because he said those words doesn't mean he was asking for more pain medication. In his current condition he could not possibly form sentences to communicate. His mind just isn't ready yet. Most likely he is experiencing a dream. However, it is a good sign that your son spoke. It means he is healing."

"But what if that's what he was trying to say? Can't you increase the dose and see what happens?"

"That's very risky. He's already at a very high dosage. There is also a risk of making him dependent on pain meds, too. I think it would be more prudent to wait and see."

But Mrs. MacIntosh would not be swayed. "No, he's my son and he needs more pain medicine. I'm sure there is still room for an increase, even if it's just for a little while. If he doesn't try to speak to us again, then you can lower the dosage. I want this for my son. Do it now!"

She was shaking with rage, fueled by love and hope.

I stood in the corner and cheered her on. "*Yeah, do it. Drug him up*."

The doctor studied her for a minute. It was a battle of will against ego.

"Very well. I will increase the dosage to its maximum

allowance for an eight hour period. Then I will lower it gradually until it is at a safe long term level. But I will only do this one time. It is not safe and it is my experience that when a patient is in a coma they will only come out of it, if ever, when they have healed enough to be able to do so.

"Although I'll admit, his speaking is very unusual, his signs all point to this being a long haul rather than a short fix. Don't take false hope from the fact he spoke. It's going to take some time for Mac to heal. And even if he does, he will require a lot of rehab and perhaps more surgery. We won't know the full extent of the damage until he does wake up. You're going to have to be patient. To rush his recovery could have fatal results. Are you willing to take that risk?"

With tears flowing, Sandra touched Mac's leg. "I just know my boy is hurt and asking for help. What if he's having trouble healing because inside his mind it's too painful to do so? What mother wouldn't want to comfort her son?" She faced the doctor and nodded. "I'm sure. Just as you said, a one-time thing."

"Yeah, stop being a dick, doc!" I shouted.

The doctor picked up the clipboard with Mac's chart and made some hasty scribbled notes. Then he turned to the nurse and told her what he ordered. Giving the family a curt nod, he left the room.

Mrs. MacIntosh and I both said, "Asshole," at the same time. I pumped my arm in a victory salute and went to check on Mac.

CHAPTER

Twenty-Nine

I found him lying perfectly still on the floor. He was barely breathing, his eyes fixed on some distant point.

My immediate concern was that he had seen the light again and it was drawing his life force to it. I didn't know how to stop him from going if he was close. I shook him, but that did no good. For all I knew I was shaking him to death.

"Mac, no! Don't go." I was in a panic and desperate. I looked heavenward. "Les!" I cried, reaching out for help.

Les' voice surrounded me. His deep, soft, confident tone calmed me. "You must make contact and soon. He is going. You may only have a few minutes to persuade him to stay."

"How?" My emotions were torn between not being able to fulfill my mission and causing Mac's premature death.

"Get next to his ear and whisper to him. Say things that will get his attention. Whatever you say has to be a stronger draw than the peaceful promises the light is offering."

My mind raced. Mac would die and it would be my fault if I didn't find a way to bring him back. I had to think fast and find something that would beat out the strength of heaven. Fat chance of that. But there was one thing that had that kind of power: love. It was my only hope. Taking a second to regroup my thoughts, I lowered my head to Mac's left ear.

"Mac, it's me, Caroline." I raised my voice in an attempt to mimic hers. "I love you, Mac. I miss you." I searched for words. "Please don't leave me. I am only a shell without you in my life. I need you to hold me. I want to feel you in my arms again. You are my soul mate and you are leaving me too soon. We will never be able to do all those wonderful things we talked about."

I didn't to go into details because I had no idea what they talked about.

"Our children will never be born. Don't you want to meet them? To grow up with them? You will miss so much."

I prayed they wanted kids. Otherwise I just blew it.

I glanced up and noticed Mac's eyes flutter briefly. He was breaking contact. I had to up the ante. I stroked the side of Mac's face and kept up a constant love fest in his ear.

Mac's eyes closed. I was winning him back, I thought. His eyes flicked open and stared past me again. "No!" I started again, stroking and whispering words of love, words no one would ever whisper to me. Words and feelings I would never get the chance to share with Monica. Somewhere in my monologue, something in me changed. Real emotion began to pour out. I sobbed and became lost in the moment, seeing Monica's angelic face instead of Mac's. It wasn't until the first tear dropped onto Mac's face that I became aware I was crying.

His eyes closed and color crept back to his face. With Monica's face in front of me, I lowered my lips down to meet hers. It was an awesome feeling, except that it wasn't her.

As our lips parted with a slight smack, Mac said, "Caroline." His arms wrapped around me and he pulled me down for another kiss. It broke my trance and as his eyes flew open, he screamed and pushed me away.

"Jesus Christ, you perv! What are you doing? Get off of me!"

I did. In a hurry.

"Aw, yuck!" He began spitting and wiping his lips. "You'd do anything to get your way, wouldn't you? How bad did you violate me?"

"I'm sorry. I was just trying to make sure you weren't dead."

"Now I wish I was. I'll be scarred for life."

"Relax. I was only giving you mouth to mouth. And-and see? It worked."

"Are you kidding me? You were kissing me."

"No I wasn't."

"That's what it felt like."

"Did you feel tongue?"

"No. Aw man, what an image."

"See, it wasn't a kiss. I only use tongue when I kiss. I'm telling you, it was mouth to mouth. What's important is that you're alive. And guess what? Your mother made the doctor give you a higher dosage of meds."

"Man, I'm not sure about doing that again."

"But you don't understand. It worked! You spoke and they heard you. Now it won't hurt as much. But you only have eight hours. If you don't go back within that time, the doctor will lower the amount again."

"I don't know, man. I have to think about this. I don't feel good. There's a lot of pressure in my head. I need to rest for a while, undisturbed. Go away. I'm afraid of what you might do when I'm asleep."

"Okay. Okay. You rest. But you did it, Mac. You did it. You should have seen Caroline's face light up when she thought you were coming back to her." All right, I fibbed a bit. She was too distraught and I really wasn't looking at her, but he didn't know that. "Stay positive. I'll be back in a bit. We have eight hours to get someone to listen to us." I was excited, but nervous about leaving him alone with his own thoughts. What if he changed his mind again?

But now that I knew Mac could communicate with his family I needed information for him to pass along. That meant going back to my death and reliving the experience. I wasn't sure I could handle seeing myself die, but I had to follow the bad guys and that was the last place where I knew they were.

CHAPTER

Thirty

"Les, it worked! It worked. It worked. It worked." I danced around in a circle with my fists pumping wildly over my head.

"I saw." He was calm. Way too calm for my liking.

"How did you see, anyway? I thought you could only see someone you had contact with."

"You wrangled your way into Mac's life. He let you in and you let me in."

"Okay, but Les, don't you see what this means? I have a chance to save those people. Why aren't you excited?"

Les shrugged.

"Come on, man. What's going on?"

"You're still messing with something that could affect a lot of people and souls. We both have a lot at stake here. I just don't think you understand the possibilities. And I mean for everyone involved."

"You're scared."

"Hell yes, I'm scared! What if word gets out that you were able to communicate with the living in this way? Can you imagine how that will affect the living and the dead? It could alter existence and afterlife. You could be solely responsible for destroying heaven and earth. Can you live with that?"

I was shocked. What I was trying could have far-reaching implications. But should that matter? If my discovery could screw up everything God had created, then

He never would have left this tiny loophole for me to find. He had to know someone would come along someday who would go looking. If I succeeded in getting a message to the living, it might cause a change in how things worked here, but I doubted it wasn't anything God couldn't handle or hadn't planned for. After all, He created me. He had to know what I was capable of.

I bit my lower lip. "I understand, Les. I do. I have to keep going. I have to believe God will forgive me. The bomb may still go off. Maybe it's what God intended all along. But if that's the case, I don't think this is the place for me."

I tilted my head back and yelled, "You hear that, God? Les has nothing to do with this! If you're the caring and loving God everyone preaches about on earth, then You'll understand why I have to do this. And please forgive Les. He's a good man. But I guess You already know that."

Les stared at me with his mouth open. He seemed to do that a lot around me. "What are you doing?"

"I'm getting you clear of this. If anyone needs to take the fall for my actions it will be me. I just have one question and I won't bother you again."

"You can't just go off on your own, interfering with other people's lives. There is a natural order to the world and sometimes bad things happen for reasons beyond our understanding."

"Bullshit."

"It's not bullshit. You are not God. You do not know His mind or His plan for all those people who might or might not die. You're messing with things you can't possibly understand."

"Isn't one of the most quoted sayings something like,

'God helps those who help themselves?' Well, I'm going to try and help those people. He can either help me help them or stay out of my way. If I fail it won't be for lack of trying. So If He doesn't like this, then He should stop me. Now, you gonna answer my question or not?"

Les mumbled, "I needed one more…just one more successful guidance and I would've been free to move on. Just one more and I had to get stuck with you."

"My question?"

"What? What else can you destroy me with?"

"You surprise me, Les. I thought your concern was for Mac. Here, all along you've been more interested in your own selfish gains. I'm disappointed."

Les' mouth fell open again. Then his eyes went all steely and his jaw snapped shut. He glared hard at me. I guess we weren't gonna be friends anymore.

"Go ahead, ask me this important question."

It was a command. I didn't much like his tone but I needed information.

"I need to follow the people who killed me. Since they interacted with me, I should be able to see and follow them, right? The question is, how?"

"You go back to the moment of your death. Picture your last memory. Once you're there you can follow them. You will not be able to interfere with them."

"That's fine. I just need to know where they are and where the bomb is going to end up." I started to leave.

"One more thing."

"Yeah?"

"The first time someone who is recently deceased watches their own death it may cause a serious emotional meltdown. It will sweep over you like an endless case of vertigo. It may take a while to regain your control and focus.

Some souls are scarred for eternity. I hope the sight doesn't affect you badly, but I do hope it affects you."

Les was gone before I could comment, which was probably for the best. I thought about what he said and tried to steel myself for the trauma. If anything, it would at least answer the question about how I died.

I brought up the vision of my fight and my opponents. I took a deep breath, closed my eyes, and jumped.

CHAPTER

Thirty-One

A solid smack to the jaw sent the tallest man down. I recognized him. He was the recipient of the flash drive; the one I stole it from. He grunted with the contact and again as he hit the cement. It was in the brief moment before the next man threw a punch that I realized we were no longer on the sidewalk. I had allowed myself to be maneuvered into the alley between the backs of a ten-story apartment building and an upscale bistro.

I ducked the next punch by the short black-haired man, grabbed the back of his head, and rammed him into the dumpster at my back. The deep bell-like clang echoed down the alley. He fell face first.

Looking toward the street, hoping to see anyone coming to the rescue had been a mistake. The third attacker decided to tackle me instead of face me head on. I would have gone down if not for the dumpster behind me. The man drop stepped, pulling us both away from the dumpster, then drove forward again. This time the impact caused a sharp pain in my back.

Before the bull of a man could smash me again, I clubbed him between the shoulder blades with joined hands; once, twice, and on the third hammer hit, I brought my knee up into his face. He slumped to the ground.

Even though the first terrorist regained his feet and was approaching me, it was here I knew the fight was over. There was one man standing on shaky legs between me and an escape. Blood dripped from his mouth. He spit and a tooth went flying. I smiled. No way was I going to be stopped.

So then why was I?

As I advanced on the tall black-haired man, the rear door of the bistro opened and a man in a suit stepped into the alley. He pulled a gun from an ankle holster and moved closer. He cast a quick glance down the alley in the opposite direction, and then stepped forward. He slid toward me as I approached the last man standing. My opponent wobbled on his feet, but suddenly stopped and froze in place. I remember thinking at the time he was afraid. His eyes went wide with fear, or so I thought. But now I realized my opponent had just seen my killer come into view from behind me.

I was so confident I was about to reach freedom I didn't notice the almost imperceptible sound the man's shoes made as he crept closer. The barrel touched the back of my head. Before I could move, the shot that ended my life was fired.

I couldn't prevent the flinch or the wave of revulsion that came over me as I watched my death play out. The gunshot flashed behind my closed eyes dozens of successive times. Even though I was already dead, coldness encompassed me. I stared at my body lying in the spreading pool of blood and shook violently. If it were possible, I would have thrown up.

I have no way of knowing how long I stood there. Had Les not come to rescue me, I might still be standing there.

He called my name several times before I blinked. Then Les stepped in front of me, shielding me from the sight of my body. “Chance! Chance!” I looked at him, my mind still reeling. “I know you had to do this. Everyone does. But I did try to warn you.”

Behind Les a man in an apron peeked out the bistro door.

Above us a woman yelled down from an apartment window, "Oh dear God, there's a body down there!" She turned back to someone inside the apartment. "I told you I heard a shot. Call the police."

Spotting the man at the door, the woman said, "Hey, check and see if that guy's still alive."

The cook stepped cautiously into the alley, looking both ways in case the killer was lurking somewhere. He saw the body--my body—and went pale. He sprinted back into the restaurant while the woman above kept calling to him.

My mouth opened but words wouldn't come out. My body vibrated like an electric current flowed through it.

"Now you know what happened. It's time to move past it." He put his hands on my shoulders. I expected to feel them there, but I felt nothing. There was no weight or pressure. "Come, let's go back."

I nodded. Even though it was only in my mind, my throat felt dry.

CHAPTER

Thirty-Two

Les led me back to my cloud. He stayed with me, trying to comfort me. Then he changed tactics.

"Okay, now you've seen for yourself. It's over and now you're here. You can take a millennium to get over your death or you can put it past you and find peace. What's it going to be?"

Though I heard him, my eyes stared straight through him, which, of course, was easy to do.

"Listen, you pain in the ass, you're the one who started this whole desperate agenda. You've probably ruined any chance you had to gain entrance to heaven and most likely jeopardized my chances as well. So what are you going to do, sit there feeling sorry for your dead ass or finish what you started?"

I blinked. The words cut through the haze and pierced my brain. Les was right. I was the one who set upon this impossible mission. People were counting on me. But Les was on a roll. Either I hadn't reacted quick enough or he was so caught up in his speech he didn't care. He went on the attack.

He was on his feet, yelling at me with his finger pointed at my face. Actually, at least the first digit was inside my face.

"You come up here with all these crazy ideas and get everyone riled up. Then just because you see your own dead body, which is why you're here in the first place, you go all weak-kneed like some little baby. Well, I'm sick of you and your stupid plans to save the world. I'm outta here. Don't call me. I won't be home."

His words angered me. When he finished yelling, I snapped my teeth at his finger. Even though there was no possible way I could have bitten him, Les yanked his hand back.

I pretended to chew and spit out his invisible finger, symbolically, of course. Les looked at his finger, making sure it was still there.

I smiled. "Made you look."

He gave me a frown meant for a misbehaving child, appropriate since that was how I was behaving.

"Okay, now what?" he asked.

"I have to go back and watch my murder again."

"Are you crazier than I thought? Look what it did to you the first time. If you are on a deadline, being comatose from shock is no way to make it."

"I'll be okay this time. I know what to expect. But I have to follow them and see where they go. One of them has to lead me to the bomb. Then I can go back and tell Mac."

"You're playing some long odds, Chance. The chances of you finding the bomb are pretty good since that part has happened already, but getting Mac to deliver the message and having his family understand what he's talking about will take a miracle."

"Well fortunately for me, I'm in the close proximity of the miracle capitol of the universe."

Les shook his head. "I hope you're right. I think a lot more than you realize depends on the outcome."

Once again I was confused, but Les did not seem compelled to explain.

CHAPTER

Thirty-Three

In a flash, I was back in the alley. As the killer touched the barrel to my head, I couldn't help it, I flinched again at the gunshot. This time, however, I didn't succumb to shock. I shook it off and forced myself to watch.

My body dropped like a stone to the pavement. I bounced once and settled. At least I hadn't felt anything. The lights went out fast.

The suit said, "Hurry, get those two up and get out of here."

The last man standing bent to help his comrades up. Meanwhile, the shooter bent next to me and began going through my pockets. He found the flash drive and slipped it into the inner pocket of his jacket.

He stood and faced the badly beaten trio. All three were bleeding. I took momentary pride in their condition. I would've won had it not been for the guy with the gun. He hadn't been man enough to face me.

Then my eyes went out of focus for a second. It hadn't been the shooter's cowardice that got me killed, but my own arrogance. No one should ever have sneaked up behind me. When you lived the kind of dangerous existence I had for so long, you didn't get cocky. You stayed cautious.

It might not have made a difference in the end. After all, the guy did have a gun, but I should've been aware of him.

When my mind refocused on the quartet, the suit was saying, "Go. When you get away from here, separate and don't call each other. Do not leave wherever you are until I tell you. You understand? I will contact you when it is time. Now go!"

The three men turned and stumbled out of the alley. On the street they scattered in different directions.

The man in the suit went in the opposite direction down the alley. I followed. Behind me a woman yelled, "Oh dear God, there's a body down there."

My killer exited the alley, turning left. He fell into a long unhurried stride. He casually looked over his shoulder. I flipped him off. I knew he couldn't see me, but the gesture made me feel better.

I followed him for several long city blocks before he turned into a restaurant. He walked toward the rear of the room and slid into a booth. After a waitress had taken his drink order, the killer took out a cell phone and made a call. While he waited to connect he slipped his other hand into his pocket and extracted the flash drive.

"Yeah, I got it. We're back in business. I'm gonna kill that fool for ever putting the information on something that could be discovered."

He listened.

"No. No problem. There's nothing to worry about. Oh, but your boys are a little banged up. The guy was tough. In fact, he was kicking their asses until I showed up. I think we got to him just in time. I'll know soon if he contacted anyone who could cause us trouble….

"Huh? No, I have no idea who he was. He wasn't a cop, I'm sure of that….

"Nope. No idea if he told anyone else. But we're going in three days anyway. There's nothing to connect us to the bomb. Your three goons might have to be eliminated, but I'll leave that to your judgment. I've done my part. Make sure the rest of my money is there. After that bomb goes off, we'll be home free and rich."

CHAPTER

Thirty-Four

I was fuming when I popped back to my cloud.

"Les!" I started pacing.

"Les!" I yelled louder.

When I turned to pace in the other direction, I literally walked into and through him. I jumped back and shivered. Nothing happened to me, but the thought of being inside him was just weird.

"You know, you are not the only person I visit. You're starting to demand too much of my attention."

"Screw that. I need your help."

"Excuse me?"

"Listen, would you? I followed the guy who shot me and if I keep following him I'll find the bomb, but in real time it will have already exploded. Is there any way to speed up the process? Can I make the thread like fast forward?"

"You amaze me, you know that?"

"Thanks, but I need an answer here."

"It wasn't a compliment. You can't speed things up like you have a TV remote. The only way to follow him now is to locate him in the present. Do you know anything about him? Do you know where he lives or what he does?"

"I don't know where he lives and what he does is blow things up."

"So you don't know where to find him. You can't just fly around browsing the streets like it's the internet. You have to know where to find him. Then you can catch him in the now."

"God Damn it!" I fumed.

"Hey!"

"Oops!" I looked up. "Sorry."

"You're losing it, you know that, Chance?"

"I said I was sorry. I'm under a lot of pressure here."

"Go follow him and find somewhere you know he might be right now. Then you can skip ahead and see if he's there in the future so you can follow him from there. It will give you a slight head's up before reality catches up."

I sighed. "Okay, Les. Thanks. I'm sorry I bothered you."

His smile showed no mirth. Then he was gone.

I jumped and was back in the restaurant watching my killer polish off a double bourbon and water. Sliding the flash drive into his jacket pocket, he tossed a twenty on the table and left. He seemed so happy with himself I wanted to smack the smile off his face.

I landed in front of him and went berserk on his body. A flurry of my punches and kicks landed and passed through him. The fact I couldn't hurt him made me try harder. Two blocks later, I was still wailing on his ass when he turned into the police station. That stopped me.

I watched as he pushed through the door. I had a very bad feeling. I followed him in, praying he would stop at the desk to ask a question, any question, even if it was just to use the bathroom. But instead he waved at the sergeant at the front desk and entered the room to the right. There he climbed a large wooden stairway and turned right where he entered a loud room full of desks with detectives and people giving statements.

My non-existent heart sank.

"Sonofabitch!" I said.

"Hipsher, where've you been, man?" A burly man sitting at a desk asked. "We're swamped here. Lend a hand, will ya?'

"No problem, O'Reilly. I'm here to save the day." He laughed and sat at a desk two down from O'Reilly. He whistled happily. I wanted to pound him further.

My killer was a cop!

CHAPTER

Thirty-Five

The shock was too much for me: I was killed by a cop. A cop! Son of a … But that meant a man charged with protecting and serving the public was about to get rich by blowing up that same public. I couldn't believe either aspect of my discovery. It was just wrong all the way around.

My obsession with stopping him increased. At least now I knew where to find him. I popped into the police station in the present. He wasn't there. I passed through every wall in the place and couldn't find him. Instead, I found two cops kissing, one smoking a joint, and another stealing a colleague's lunch, but no Hipsher.

I was pissed and confused. Should I go searching for him or wait until he showed up, even though it was costing me precious time? What if he was out placing the bomb? Or worse, what if he left town to avoid the blast? I'd never find him then.

I went back to his desk and sat in his chair. As I tried to puzzle out the best solution an idea sprang to mind. I popped back in time three hours. The room changed slightly. Most of the same detectives were there but the people they were helping had changed. There was still no Hipsher.

I tried again.

Three more hours and there were fewer people on the floor. Two policemen came in escorting a rough-looking man in handcuffs who needed convincing to have a seat. They managed to convince him, but he bled on the detective's desk.

Three more hours back and still no sign of my prey. I was beginning to fear I had lost him and would have to go back to the last time I saw him at the station. That could really put me behind, especially if I had to follow him around for a long period of time to establish his routine.

I tried once more.

He wasn't there. I banged my head against his desk, which was easier to do now since it no longer hurt.

O'Reilly's voice thundered over the din. "Hipsher, you've got to be kidding me! Seriously, man, where you going now?"

Hipsher stood at the door and blew a kiss to O'Reilly. "Try not to miss me too much. I'd hate for you to get so worked up you might explode." He laughed, waved, and walked out the door. Several fellow officers sent him a one-finger goodbye salute of their own.

"Can you believe that guy?" O'Reilly said to the others. Some shook their heads. One said, "He needs to move on to another precinct."

I was the only one in the room who understood Hipsher's reference to exploding. I was also the only one who could stop him. I literally flew after him.

Hipsher strutted down the crowded sidewalk wearing a smug expression. He nodded to passers-by and turned his head to ogle several women. He even whistled at one. Hipsher was having the time of his life.

In the next block he entered a parking garage. On the second floor, Hipsher stopped at a newer red Dodge Charger and fobbed it open. He slid in and locked the door. Glancing over his shoulders to make sure no one was lurking around, he pulled out his phone and made a call.

"Okay, we're all set. No one has come forward with knowledge about a bomb threat. Your boys should have the device. I've given them instructions on how to set the timer. They know the location and I expect have worked out the logistics. I will contact you after it's done. That will be the last time we speak. I plan on being a long way off by the time things begin to happen...

"Na, na. Just listen. Here's the thing. After the timer's set and the device is placed in position, you will have a half hour to deposit my money. You got that? A half hour. If I can't get my money by then I will turn the timer off and place an anonymous call to the police detailing where the bomb is. Are we understood?"

He listened for a moment then a look of annoyance crossed his face. "I'm not doing this for free. I don't care what your ideology is, what your goals are, your message, or who you're trying to avenge. I want the rest of my money. We clear?"

"Good. I'll call you. Ciao."

He tossed the phone on the passenger seat and started the car. I was in the back seat as he pulled out of the parking structure and turned west toward the suburbs. "Okay, Abdullah, you'd better not screw me," he said to himself. "You don't know who I am, but I sure as hell know who you are. Just follow the plan and everything will go smooth. Yeah, two cool million coming my way."

I wrapped my arm around his neck and squeezed for all I was worth—which, as a ghost, wasn't much. However, I was pleasantly surprised when the hairs on the back of his neck stood up and he rubbed the spot. His eyes flicked a few times in my direction. He looked a little nervous.

He shook his head. "Don't lose it now, Bradley. You don't want to miss out on your big payday." He turned on the radio, but from time to time still glanced in the rear view mirror.

Somehow I had an effect on him. He felt my presence. Now if I could figure out a way to increase that feeling, maybe I could cause him to panic and make a mistake. Then again, it could just be my imagination, but at this point I was willing to try anything.

CHAPTER

Thirty-Six

I stayed with him all the way to his house. There I watched him pack two large duffel bags with clothes and then go around the house collecting things he wanted to take with him. Now that I knew where he would be, I was going back to Mac and try to get the word out. Then I would pop back here in the morning and follow Hipsher to the bomb.

The drugs should've had time to work on Mac's body by then. I jumped straight to his brain's hiding place. It was empty. The room seemed somewhat smaller than it had been the last time I visited. Then I realized Mac had erected walls to keep me away from him.

Exasperated, I threw my hands in the air. "Ah, Mac, I thought we'd worked this all out. Come on, man, I've got a lot of information for you to send back. Are you gonna help or not?"

No answer.

"Look, you already know I'm not going to stop. I can't. It's not in my makeup. I have to try and if that means wasting the few hours I have left to tear these walls down, then that's what I'm gonna do. Now, come on. You already agreed to try. Don't make me go through the reasons why it's important again. Be brave. Be strong. Be out here in a minute or I'm gonna lose my patience."

When nothing happened, I attacked the first wall with such fierce power that it began to sway with the first blows.

"Okay, okay! Stop! Don't destroy everything. I'm here.

I'll help."

Mac walked into the open and the walls disappeared. He raised his arms to his sides in defeat. "What do you want me to do?"

"I'm not sure how long you will be able to stay in your body. Hopefully it's long enough to get out a message. Repeat it if you can, then get back out so you don't endure pain or risk permanent damage. We're gonna have to do this several times so I don't want it to be traumatic for you."

"I like how you say '*we're*' gonna do this several times."

"Hey, believe me, I wish I could change places with you—if only to be able to see the world again. You don't understand how much power that thought has to me. You're lucky. You may still live but I'll never have that chance again. So to be able to trade places with you for only a moment would be amazing."

"I'm sorry. I never looked at it that way before. I'll do my best. I promise."

"I'm not trying to kill you here. I really pray you will get healthy and live a long and happy life. I do. Just not this moment, okay?"

Mac smiled and nodded. "What do you want me to say?"

I had thought about that very question for a while. The best way to get his family's attention would be to mention the bomb. "Start off saying 'bomb'. Repeat it a few times. 'There's a bomb. There's a bomb.' Say 'cops'."

"'Cops'?"

"Yeah, it looks like a cop is behind the plot. He's also my killer."

"Wait, a cop killed you? Are you sure you weren't a criminal?"

My anger began to rise. I fought to keep cool. "I won't

deny I did some things that weren't entirely legal, but they were for the right reasons and to protect innocent people from some bad situations. I'm not gonna stand here and try to justify my life to you. This cop snuck up behind me, placed his gun against my head, and shot me. He is gonna set off a bomb somewhere still to be determined sometime tomorrow night.

"Regardless who is involved, the explosion still has to be stopped. Agreed? This is a terrorist action against our country and a cop is helping them do it."

"Yeah, okay. Anything else?"

"You can mention my name, Chance Swift, and that the bomb will explode tomorrow."

"Can I say hi to my mom and fiancée?"

"Of course, but please say the rest first so you don't get sidetracked."

"Let's do this." Mac said and extended his hand.

I shook it.

Mac took a couple long deep breaths, looked at me, and vanished. Panicked, I forgot to get into the room first, so I blinked into my usual corner just in time to see Mac's face scrunch up in pain.

Caroline was the first to see the change and came to her feet.

"Mac! Oh Mac, baby, are you okay?"

His mother ran to the other side of the bed. "He looks like he's in such pain. Quick, get a nurse," she commanded her husband. He bolted through the door.

Mac's mouth worked to open but apparently it was a struggle to do so.

"Ba. Ba. Ba."

"What, honey? What are you trying to say?" Caroline asked.

The door opened. A nurse, whose name tag said, 'Beverly' came in, followed by Barney. She was quick to the bedside, wearing a curious expression.

Mac's mother said, "He's trying to speak, but can't get the words out."

Seeing Mac's contorted features, Beverly first checked the IV drip and his vitals. Then she opened a drawer and pulled out what looked like a pack of large blue colored Q-tips. She tore the package open, withdrew one, and wiped it inside Mac's mouth and along his gums.

"What is that?" asked the mother.

"It's just to moisturize the mouth. With the medications and the amount of time he's been asleep, his mouth is dry."

"Bomb."

"What?" asked Caroline, her face scrunched up with confusion.

"Bomb"

"What, dear?" his mother leaned closer. "What's he talking about, 'bomb'?"

"Explosion."

The room went silent.

"Tomor. Tomor. Bomb."

"He must be dreaming," Mr. MacIntosh said.

"Chance. Bomb. Must save."

Then Mac was unconscious again.

The voices in the room exploded like a bomb as everyone began talking at once.

"Bomb? What does that mean?" Mac's mother said.

"Is he delirious? Does he have a fever?" Caroline asked the nurse.

"It had to be a dream," his father added.

CHAPTER

Thirty-Seven

Beverly listened to the family go on about Mac's words. The she got lost in her own thoughts, trying to ignore the noise while she continued to examine Mac. *Wow!* She thought. It's very unusual for a comatose patient to wake up and speak, then go back under. It's usually all or nothing. When the other nurses told her Mac spoke, she had her doubts. There was no denying what she heard, but what did it mean?

Was he deep in a dream state or was this Mac involved in something bad when he was alive? Or … ? But was any of what he said true? Could she take the chance it was just a dream? What had he said about the bomb, tomor? Did that mean tomorrow?

Beverly finished her assessment. "His heart rate has returned to normal. His color looks better too. He doesn't appear to have a fever. To be honest, I've never seen this happen before. It could be a dream; I'm not sure. I think it's a good sign that he spoke, regardless of what was said. I'll make a report for the doctor. In the meantime, keep up the prayers and talk to him. I'll return shortly." She smiled at Mac's mother, putting a hand on hers. "I think the extra meds helped."

Mrs. MacIntosh nodded while her tears streamed. Nurse Beverly walked out of the room. I followed. Her reactions and mannerisms after Mac's words made me think, if anyone would do something, it would be her. She stopped at the nurses station.

"What's the commotion this time?" an older, heavyset woman named Bethany, asked.

Nurse Beverly was in a trance, gazing off down the hall.

"Bev?" said Todd, a tall, thin male nurse.

"Huh? Oh! He spoke again."

"What do you mean, spoke?" A short black nurse, Tanya asked.

"That's what he did. I heard him. I was in the room when he talked."

"That's amazing!" exclaimed Bethany. "So is he awake?"

"No, he just said a few words then was gone again."

Todd said, "What words? Did they make sense?"

"Yes and no. He said, 'bomb, explosion' and a word that sounded like 'tomorrow.' I'm not sure what it means."

"Sounds like he's remembering the motorcycle accident. To him it would've been like an explosion," Todd said.

"But what would tomorrow have to do with it? The accident already happened."

"Girl, I haven't a clue. Has anyone ever seen someone in a coma come out of it before?" Tanya said.

Bethany responded, "I have several times. Usually they aren't as banged up as this guy though, and they've only been out a few days. This is what, his fourth or fifth day here?"

"Yeah," said Beverly. "Do you think I should call someone, you know, about the bomb thing?"

"I don't," said Bethany. "It can't be about anything real."

Tanya added, "And why you want to get the police involved and get that poor boy's family all riled up? The police just gonna think he's the bomber. In that condition he ain't gonna be blowing nobody up."

"Honey," Bethany said, "It's just a coma induced dream. Don't give the words any meaning. The important thing is that he spoke. That's a good thing."

"I don't know," said Todd. "You can't be too careful nowadays. What if there really is a bomb and this guy's trying to warn us?"

"Oh Todd, you been watching too much sci-fi. You think he's in touch with someone from the other side who's trying to warn us? You crazy."

"Well, stranger things have happened," he replied, becoming defensive.

They laughed. Bev smiled, but I could see her wheels turning.

"Maybe aliens have his mind and are messing with us," Tanya said.

"Hey, that's not funny," said Todd. "That could really happen."

Tanya walked down the hall, "Like I said—crazy."

Bethany walked into an office, leaving Todd and Beverly.

"Do you really think it could be something, Todd?"

"I don't know, Bev. But what if it is real and you did nothing?" He frowned and walked away, leaving Bev to think. I only wished I could read her mind to see what she was going to do.

CHAPTER

Thirty-Eight

Mac was weak, but not nearly as torn up as he had been after the previous attempts. The extra dose of drugs had helped enough to enable him to break through and stay for a longer time. All I could do was hope it would make convincing him to go back a lot easier. And since Nurse Bev hadn't called anyone with her information, it looked like Mac would have to go back.

Sitting on the floor of his cocoon, I cradled Mac in my arms while he recovered. His hand was pressed to his forehead.

"It wasn't as bad this time. There's a throbbing in my head, but nothing like the first time."

"Good. I don't want you to be in pain."

"No, but what's a little long term headache, huh?"

"I wish there was another way, but hey, you did it. They heard you and you got a response."

"I didn't get to speak to Caroline, though. My throat was so dry I couldn't get the words to come out. It wasted too much time."

"Maybe now that they heard you speak they'll keep your mouth moist. It'll make speaking easier and you can say more."

"Next time, huh? You really do want to kill me, don't you?"

"Don't say that. I don't want you die. But now that you know you can communicate, don't you think the risk is worth the reward?"

"You keep saying that, but I think my only reward will be death."

"Yeah, but just think about it: then you'll be able to spend all your time with me." I flashed a huge smile to show I was kidding, but in the back of my mind I thought, if I'm still here when you get here.

"I know you're hurting, even though the pain isn't as bad, but I have to go. I need to see if what you said is being passed along to someone who can help us. Your nurse looks like the best bet. I'll be back later after you're rested so we can try again."

"There goes that we thing again. Don't hurry back."

I lowered him to the floor. He could still feel pain so I set him down gently. Then I shot back into the hospital room to listen to the chatter. The family was still talking to each other and to Mac. They kept asking him to come back and explain what he meant about the bomb. Mac's mother looked strong, but doubt had crept into Caroline's eyes.

Sandra and Caroline talked about if Mac actually had some connection to a bomb. Their voices were rising. Barney kept saying, "Calm down. It didn't mean anything. It was just a dream. You don't want Garrett to hear you two fighting, do you?"

I didn't like his response.

I went out to find Nurse Beverly. She was bustling about, doing her rounds. The way her brows stayed knitted together meant something was on her mind, or maybe that was just my hope. I jumped back and forth for hours, waiting to see if any-thing happened.

Depression had long ago taken over my demeanor. After the second hour, hope had faded. I was afraid to go back and tell Mac we failed. Of course, if I told him that, it would give him a good excuse not to try again. No; for the time being I decided to keep that bit of information to myself.

When Nurse Beverly left at the end of her shift, she took the last of my hopes with her.

I went back into the room, sat in Sandra's chair, and flopped my head into my hands. I had to regroup. Whatever Mac said the next time had to grab their attention enough that they would react. I also had to protect Mac, so I wanted to make sure one of the first things he said was to keep the drugs coming. The less pain he experienced, the more likely I could talk him into trying again and probably again.

The time was ticking away. Sometime tomorrow a bomb would be detonated. I had about 24 hours to stop it. That would've been hard enough to do if I were alive.

CHAPTER

Thirty-Nine

"Hey Mike, what's shaking?"

"Nothing much, Jimbo. Still trying to put together the pieces of this latest homicide."

Jim O'Reilly slipped into his jacket as he hit the stairs. Michael Pollen was on his way out too.

"So, whatcha got so far?"

"Guy got mugged and killed by two or more attackers, except nothing was missing. His wallet with two hundred cash, a watch, and car keys were still on him. One pocket was turned out like maybe they grabbed something, but it's hard to say what."

"Got anything else?"

"Not much. Blood from three others besides the deceased. One tooth, some hair. Witness upstairs heard a dumpster 'dong'."

"Dong?"

"As she puts it. You know, like a bell but deeper. She went to her window but she moves slow. Then she heard the shot. When she looked out her window she caught the tail-end of a guy in a sport coat disappear around the corner of the alley. Only description was the jacket was light brown."

The two men exited the building and started down the street for the parking garage.

"Huh! Sounds like a tough one."

"Yeah, aren't they all? Well, most."

"Who's the vic?"

"Some former medal-winning Ranger. Guess he made his living by helping people with serious problems. The few people I've found who knew him had nothing but praise for him. Nice guy who always was willing to lend a hand. Helped a woman who was being abused by her husband. Helped a rape victim, helped a blackmail victim; even recovered a kidnapped kid."

"Huh! Sounds like he pissed someone off who had him dealt with. Find his latest client and you may find the killer."

"Yeah, thought of that. Problem is, all his so-called clients aren't written down in any case files. He was strictly off the books."

O'Reilly opened the door to the parking garage stairs and started up.

"The hard part is finding where this guy lived. There's no record of him anywhere. With the money he was carrying and the way he looked, he wasn't living on the streets. I'm meeting with one of his clients now who may be able to point me in the right direction." Pollen opened the third floor door and they started across the floor. Pollen asked, "What're you working on?"

O'Reilly laughed. "Ah, nothing really; just doing a favor for a friend."

"A favor, huh? So un-job related?"

"No, actually I guess it is, if it's real."

They stopped at O'Reilly's car.

"Well, now you got me curious."

O'Reilly laughed and held up a hand. "Got a call from a nurse friend of mine. She's got a guy in a coma where she works. Guess he got slammed in a motorcycle accident and may not make it. But anyway, out of the clear blue, the guy starts babbling about a bomb."

"Whoa! Seriously? He wakes up and spews out about a bomb? Did he build it and suddenly feel guilty about it?"

"No, that's the thing. He never wakes up. He just starts talking. Says something about it blowing up tomorrow."

"So it's a dream."

"That's what I'm thinking. Anyway, it spooked Bev pretty bad so I told her I'd stop by."

"So it's off the caseload; you're just doing it for a friend."

"Well, sorta. She's a looker. I told her I'd look, but she had to go to dinner with me."

"Jimbo, you dog, you."

"Yeah, but it worked. Funny though, I'd been thinking about her lately—wondering what she's been doing. Kinda strange, huh?"

"Hey, it's fate. Well, good luck to you. Hope it all works out."

"Yeah, thanks. Good luck catching your killer."

Pollen waved and walked to his own car, thinking about what O'Reilly had said. He laughed at the big man's dinner ploy, happy at least someone had a date. Good for O'Reilly.

CHAPTER

Forty

I was about to give up my vigil and go see how Mac was recovering when the door opened and Nurse Beverly entered the room. She was all dressed up and looking quite fine. A big man in an ill-fitting sport coat followed her in. He looked familiar somehow.

The family members stood with surprised expressions.

"Caroline, Mr. and Mrs. MacIntosh, this is a friend of mine, Detective Jim O'Reilly. I told him about your son's remarkable recovery and what he said, and he would like to ask you some questions if that would be all right."

Instantly I perked up. Now I recognized him. He knew and disliked Hipsher. That made him an ally as far as I was concerned. Yay, Bev.

They looked to each other and Mrs. MacIntosh answered, "I guess, but my son didn't do anything wrong. He's not in trouble, is he?"

"No ma'am. I'm here more out of curiosity than anything else. But I hope you understand the mention of the word 'bomb' makes people nervous, so I decided to check it out."

"I don't understand," said Caroline. "Did she call the police about a dream?" She was agitated and looked ready to defend her man.

Nurse Beverly tensed up, visibly on edge.

"No, ma'am," Big Jim said. His voice was soft as if trying to ease the tension. "Miss Hoyt and I were having dinner and she told me about a near miracle recovery by your son. She was very excited and hoped that his words were a sign that he would come out of his coma soon. I asked what he said and decided to check it out. She didn't call me, I kinda insisted, so don't blame her."

Beverly relaxed after the explanation. She smiled warily at the family, but positively beamed at Detective O'Reilly.

The family members still seemed a little apprehensive, but backed off and allowed O'Reilly to advance toward the bed. Watching Caroline, I still feared she might pounce.

"So this is Garrett, eh? It was a motorcycle accident?"

"Yes," Mrs. MacIntosh said. "Another driver pulled in front of him. Our poor boy. He's so-so broken." She started to cry.

O'Reilly turned to Barney. "Mr. MacIntosh, can you tell me what your son said?"

"Yeah, but I wasn't in the room for some of it. I went to get the—her." He gestured toward Beverly.

Mrs. MacIntosh cleared her throat. Her voice shaking, she repeated word for word what Garrett had said.

"Can anyone else add anything to that or do you all agree with what was said?"

"Nope, that was it as far as I remember," the father said.

"I agree," added Caroline. "Except even though he was talking he couldn't seem to open his eyes. Garrett looked as though he were in pain. That must be why when he woke up the last time he asked for drugs." She put her hand to her mouth and started to cry. "He's trying to come back to us but it must hurt too much."

O'Reilly turned to Nurse Beverly. "He talked before?"

She shrugged. "I wasn't here at the time, but that's what I was told. It makes a certain amount of sense if he is trying to regain consciousness that he might ask for an increased amount of pain medication. Of course, his body can only handle so much. His doctor said that without knowing what's going on inside it's hard to determine what's best for him. But he did increase the dose a bit."

Caroline wiped at her eyes. "What if the dose were increased again? Maybe he could come back and stay."

"You'll have to discuss that with his doctor. It's certainly worth exploring, but you have to understand, Garrett has serious injuries. His coma is self-induced in order for him to recover. He won't wake up until his body and his mind agree that it's safe for him to do so. If he's on drugs it might help him to wake up, but the drugs will mask the pain and still make him suffer. We don't want him addicted. When he's ready, he'll come back."

O'Reilly interrupted. "Let's get back to this bomb. Does your son have any knowledge of bomb making? Or maybe know anyone who has?"

"No, of course not," the mother said.

Barney stepped forward, his anger flaring. "I don't like the direction you're going with this. My son had a nightmare and uttered a word. The next thing we know, he's under investigation. I think you should leave." He looked at Beverly. "And maybe we should have another nurse look after Garrett from now on. Preferably someone that doesn't blab our business all over the city. Aren't there regulations that prevent you from doing that? I'm going to report this to the hospital administrators."

Beverly's lip quivered. O'Reilly noticed and put a comforting arm around her. "There won't be any need for that. Your son is not under investigation. I was merely curious. I hope your son gets well soon."

Oh no! He was about to leave. This wasn't going as I had hoped. I beamed back to Mac's brain.

"Mac, you have to go back."

"I'm not sure I'm ready yet. My head still hurts."

"You have to." My desperation made me too demanding, but we had to react in haste. "There's a detective in your room right now." Mac lifted his head. Your dad's chasing him away. This could be our only chance. We have to take it."

He pushed himself up from the floor. "I sure wish you'd stop with all this we stuff." He looked up then toward me. "This is going to hurt, isn't it?"

"I'm sorry."

He frowned and disappeared. I was right behind him.

O'Reilly's large back was exiting the door. *Oh, God Mac, hurry!* Caroline was still crying. Mac's father was still fuming. Fortunately, Sandra was looking at her son.

Mac's face contorted and he gasped. The meds must have worn off. He struggled to break free.

"He's trying again!" his mother exclaimed.

I looked at the doorway and it was empty. Barney ran through it, I presumed, to fetch a nurse, as was usual.

Caroline tore a moist stick from the pack and jammed in Mac's mouth. She swished it around and pulled it out just as the night shift nurse entered.

"He needs more pain medication," Sandra said.

The nurse checked the IV bag. It was still a quarter full. "He's not scheduled for more for another hour."

"I don't care! He needs it now!" Sandra shouted. The nurse blinked hard from shock. "Let me contact the doctor and see what he says. I'm not allowed to give him more on my own."

She left the room but had to move through O'Reilly and Beverly who had crowded back into the doorway.

Mac's father yelled, "I thought I told you to leave!"

His wife shushed him.

O'Reilly raised a hand to show he was going then froze as Mac's ragged voice quieted the room.

"Bomb. Tomorrow. Ah. Hurts. Cop. Swift. Killed. Al. Bomb. Help. Hurts."

And that was all that Mac could take.

I looked toward O'Reilly with the ultimate of great expectations. He was jotting something down in a notepad that seemed lost in his large hand. His eyebrows were raised at an angle indicating thought or maybe confusion. On me it would have indicated constipation, but I didn't think that fit here. Although he did say they had just come from dinner.

"I got 'bomb, tomorrow, hurts, cop, swift, killed, Al, bomb, help, and hurts.' Anything else? Did I miss something?"

Beverly replied, "I-I don't think so."

"Garrett, honey," his mother said, "Are you still there? Is this a dream or are you trying to tell us something? Talk to me, sweetie."

Beverly said, "But what does it mean?"

"If anything," O'Reilly finished.

CHAPTER

Forty-One

I watched O'Reilly study the words he wrote as he and Beverly walked down the hall. This big detective was the key now. He had to believe in what he heard and act on it. I had to admit, it really wasn't much to go on. Still, it was a start.

I followed them down the elevator. It was Beverly who brought up the subject.

"Jim, do you believe in life after death?"

"You mean like heaven and hell and the existence of God?"

"Well, sort of, but more... hmm—let me ask you this, do you believe in the soul?"

"Ah, yeah, I guess, but I don't think I want to hear where this is going."

She gave him a frown. "No, really. Listen to me, please. There are a lot of people who believe that once the soul leaves the body, it just hovers over the world. What if Garrett is in contact with someone from the other side who is trying to pass information to us?"

"No, I'm not going there, Bev. I'm a detective. I've been trained to believe in the facts. To find clues. Those are real things that you can see and prove. I can't believe in what I can't prove. I'm sorry."

"So, you're not opened minded enough to even consider the possibility?"

"Aw, gee, don't make it sound like a bad thing. I can't

help the way I am."

"And here I thought I was going to like you."

"Bev, please. I had a really good time tonight. Let's not ruin it by disagreeing over this."

"If you truly had a good time, this discussion shouldn't be able to ruin it. And if I can so easily ruin a good time for you because we disagree over something, I don't think there's a ghost of a chance this relationship can develop. So maybe it's for the best."

"Yeah. Nice choice of words."

The elevator landed and the doors slid open. Beverly quick stepped ahead. "Bev, what do you want me to do?" O'Reilly hurried to catch her. "There's no crime anywhere. All I have are a few words spoken by a guy in a coma. Where do I go from here?"

"You're the detective; you tell me."

"This is crazy. How do I interview a ghost, especially if don't believe in them."

Stopping abruptly, Beverly was almost trampled as O'Reilly ran into her. He grabbed her arms to keep her from falling. She looked from hand to hand then up into his ruggedly handsome face. He had strong hands and arms. In school, she had wanted to be held in those arms, but that had been so long ago. That had been a school girl's crush. She'd had no expectations that her daydreams would ever become reality. Yet, here they were.

"Let's say that you learned all about me and I learned all about you. We liked what we found out enough to take it to the next level."

O'Reilly swallowed hard. "You mean sex?"

She frowned. "No, dummy; marriage. Stay with me here. We got married and were living the happy ever after thing.

Then one day I came home with this story and was all concerned and upset about it. I asked you to look into it for me and would be happy with whatever you found out." She paused for effect.

O'Reilly swallowed the hook and said, "And?"

"Would you love me enough to take my word for what occurred and at least look into it?"

He was caught and knew it. His smile was weak. It took a moment, but his answer came out as any man's would who had hopes of love. "Yes, for you I would."

She brushed his hands off and turned toward the outer door. "Well, then, if you want a chance a second date and wherever that may lead in the future, you'll pretend we're married now and look into it."

He stood there, watching her exit. A big smile spread across his face.

From the door, Beverly called over her shoulder, "You know, you're not winning any points here by making me open my own door."

O'Reilly laughed and jogged after her.

At the car, he opened the door for Bev and she said, "Hurry up, stud. Your evening's not over yet."

I liked Beverly. All I could do was hope O'Reilly liked her enough to check it out. I would've followed them further, but was afraid of what I might see.

CHAPTER

Forty-Two

When I blinked back to Mac, it was difficult to gain entrance to his mind. The cone of light was faint and narrow where it connected to the earth. I remembered Les telling me that if the light ever lost contact with earth, that soul had died and was moving on.

I feared for Mac. I didn't want him to die, but if he did, I really didn't want it to be my fault. When I finally made it into his consciousness, I found Mac on the floor going through violent spasms. I threw myself on the floor beside him and scooped his body up into my lap.

"Oh God Mac, I'm so sorry. I didn't know the drugs would wear off that soon. You were so good. You fought so hard. Please don't give up yet. We're so close. I think they're talking about raising the dosage even more. It'll be easier next time."

I wasn't sure he could hear me through all the pain, but I kept talking anyway. Hopefully, my voice and words were comforting and reassuring and not adding to his agony. I was well aware of the fact that before I showed up Mac had probably never experienced this kind of pain. At least his body and mind were able to separate from the after the accident. The coma protected him from feeling the physical pain but there was no protection from this. I was making him weaker and possibly unable to regain his body and have a life.

I was trapped. Unable to stop trying to save the lives of

the potential bomb victims, but to stop the explosion, I may end up sacrificing the one person who could save them. One way or the other I was going to live with a lot of guilt. In fact, it had already started to pile up.

I'm not sure how long I rocked Mac, but eventually he calmed and his brain slept. I left him then and went back to my new home to think about what I had done and to plan out what I would continue to do. I wasn't a good person. I looked around at my cloud-like apartment. I'd better not get used to it. I wouldn't be here long.

* * *

Michael Pollen couldn't believe how hard it had been to track down information about Chance Swift. After meeting with a very reluctant client he found by going through the Swift's cell phone records, Pollen came away with a different perspective of the murder victim.

It seemed that Swift hired himself out to desperate people who themselves were victims of some sort. In this case, the wealthy, middle-aged couple had hired Swift through an intermediary to deliver money to a kidnapper. The kidnap victim was an eight month old baby girl—the couple's only child. They had been afraid to contact the police. They found Swift through a family member who had used him to stop a blackmailer.

Although they were nervous to be talking to a police detective, they did nothing but sing Swift's praises. They were visually upset by the news he was dead. It did, however, ease their consciences about telling his tale.

Evidently Swift had not only brought back their daughter safe and unaffected by her ordeal, but had returned the money as well. They were shocked. Swift's response to the couple's queries had been, 'It's better you don't know. It's over and done. You will have nothing to fear from them again.' They didn't push the issue further.

They offered the ransom money to Swift as a bonus, but he accepted only his fee and ten percent of the money. Pollen left there with a grudging respect for the man, even though he still thought of him as a criminal.

The couple had not known the man's name although their description matched Swift. However, Pollen did leave there with the name and phone number of the family member who'd passed along Swift's name. From that man, he got the name of the husband's uncle, who had been blackmailed for something he refused to discuss. From him, Pollen learned the name of the intermediary involved. A man named Roberts acted as the agent for Swift, who the uncle knew as Morgan. Swift had an alias; probably more than one.

Leaving the uncle, Pollen had a description of Roberts and a better understanding of how the operation worked. In essence, Swift/Morgan was a hero for hire, like Spenser from the novels. He was an underground do-gooder; a vigilante, although Pollen held no illusions as to the fate of the criminals Swift hunted down. Swift had been a dangerous and deadly man who obviously used his military training to his benefit.

He headed back to the office to run searches because even with the information he had gathered, Pollen felt no closer to finding Swift's killers. He needed to find Swift's residence or his partner Roberts. There could've been a lot of reasons Swift was killed. He might have run into friends of those he had dealt with before or he might have been on a new mission to help someone. That bothered him the most because it meant someone else; someone who had been desperate enough to contact Swift, was still in need of help.

His discoveries shocked and amazed him that so many people turned to a troubleshooter rather than the police. He could understand why to some extent, but the thought saddened him, because it spoke to how ineffectual the law could be.

Whatever the case, Pollen was sure Swift's death was something beyond a simple mugging gone wrong. It was just a gut reaction, but Pollen couldn't shake the feeling that time was of the essence. Someone's life was in danger. Now it was up to him to piece together whatever Swift had been working on, and fast.

He sighed. He had so little to work with. He could only hope the computer would give him a direction before it was too late for whatever.

CHAPTER

Forty-Three

While I waited for Mac to recover, I decided to ride the thread that led to my wife again. I couldn't stop thinking about her and the life we would never have. The image I had of Monica wasn't clear enough in my mind. Of course, that was just an excuse to see her again.

I landed at the diner in the thread of our happy meeting and sat at our booth. I avoided the reality thread, the one that continued in the real world after my death. I wasn't sure I wanted to know about her life without me.

I watched her work. She was beautiful and I longed for her like the lost love she was. If only I could touch her, just once. To stroke her hair, caress her cheek, or hold her close to me. It was easy to get caught up in the 'if onlys.' My mood swung from elation to depression.

I followed her like an invisible puppy. Several minutes later the real version of me walked in. Watching the interaction between her and me made me smile yet caused an aching in my heart. I wasn't sure about how Monica felt, but for me it was love at first sight. If this was what it was like to meet the woman of my dreams, I was saddened to have missed it.

I followed Monica and my luckier self on the walk home. Again we passed the alley. The druggies and the man I bashed into the dumpster were still there. My lip curled up like an agitated dog's. I wanted a piece of that guy, bad.

At Monica's apartment we stopped and talked in that

nervous first date way that couples did, not wanting the night to end and wondering about a good night kiss. Or maybe that was my take on it, since we weren't really on a date. We did, however, agree to meet the next day at the diner. Both mes were elated. Observing the scene was strange. I experienced the happy couple's interaction as if watching two strangers, yet I felt their emotions as if I were actually involved.

I left Monica and the luckier me there in their awkwardness. I wanted to see what the future held for us. I discovered I could skip ahead. Evidently, as long as it wasn't reality you could skip through the possible variations of your life at warp speed. I stopped one month later. We were holding hands as we walked to her apartment. We no longer stopped at the front steps. Now we climbed to the third floor and entered her apartment. From there I found just how far our relationship had gone. Yes, and God forgive me, I watched.

Six months later the relationship had grown stronger. We moved in together. I gave up my wild and dangerous lifestyle and tried to help people in a much safer way. I did odd jobs and a lot of volunteer work, but that never made us much money. Fortunately, I still had money hidden away from my previous work. It lasted until shortly after we were married. I splurged on a honeymoon to Hawaii. We were happy, but it didn't take long for the stress of my unemployment to become a daily topic. We struggled and sometimes argued over our finances and our future. I took on menial jobs that I hated but brought in supplemental money.

Then, one day, almost two years later, our lives changed forever. After another money fight, I was out walking when I stumbled across a mugging. I slowed down the whirlwind tour of my never-to-be-realized life so I could see what was happening.

It was three against one and reminded me of my own past ordeal. Without hesitation, I used my pent up anger to hammer my way into the mayhem. When the bloodlust cleared from my vision, the three thugs were down and out and the victim was leaning up against a wall, holding his nose.

Panting like a mad dog, I turned to him. The man I saved held up a hand in defense while blood dripped down the other. I realized he was afraid of me. The last of my anger bled away.

"Are you all right?" I asked.

"Yeah."

"You want me to call the police?"

He shook his head. "Can you just get me out of here without anyone seeing us?"

I thought about his request for a second, surveying the damage I had caused. "Move down to the other end of the alley. I've got an old blue Blazer. I'll pull it up, you hop in."

He nodded and I ran off to fetch my vehicle.

To my surprise he directed me to the ballpark. The security guard motioned us through when he recognized my passenger. Though intrigued, I grew anxious because I had no idea who he was.

Later, I found out the man I rescued was all-star Yankee third baseman Mickey Strauss. To thank me, he brought me into the locker room where he introduced me to some of the team. I was allowed to sit on the bench during the game, and afterward Mickey took me to dinner at his favorite steakhouse. We talked for a long time and after hearing my current employment status, he hired me as his driver and bodyguard. After all this time, I finally made it to the big leagues. I made a friend for life and more importantly scored a steady paycheck for a long time— a really big paycheck.

CHAPTER

Forty-Four

Skipping ahead again I saw Monica and myself move into a large suburban house. The sparkle had returned to her eyes and I was happy to be her hero again. We had three great kids. Mickey and I became close friends. I got to hang around a major league ballpark and players. When Mickey retired, the club offered me a job as kind of a troubleshooter to keep some of their players out of the public eye. That part wasn't as much fun and five years later I retired.

My oldest son, Mickey, became a good baseball player. He was a star in high school. My second child, Aby, looked just like her mother. She was a definite heartbreaker. As a freshman in high school, she starred in the school musical. I was blown away by her voice and the emotion in her eyes.

Dominic was the serious one. He was a good athlete, but was also a straight A student. He worried me, though. He looked like me and had an unsettled vibe about him. I didn't want him to follow in my footsteps. Look where that got me.

Monica had asked me why I wanted Dominic for his name. I explained it was to honor an old friend of mine, but I never told her much more than that. Since I stopped being a gun for hire, Dominic had disappeared.

While working for Mickey, he introduced me to his financial consultants who took my money and made it grow like they planted it in fertile soil and watered it daily. When I retired from the team, Mickey hired me for a nothing position in his corporation. Evidently he just liked having me around. And although I felt guilty about taking his money for nothing, I still took it until his death twelve years later.

I stopped watching then. I wanted to have those happy memories to last me for eternity. There was no sense going through the sadness of watching Monica and the kids die.

When I shut down the movie of my possible future, I sighed. I would've had a sweet life. It was sad that I never got to live it, but I was happy to have seen it. It felt good knowing a bum like me could've actually amounted to something. I never met Monica. With me dead, the kids would never exist. But they were part of me and I loved them as if they were real.

CHAPTER

Forty-Five

"Now remember, you promised to keep an open mind," Beverly admonished.

"Okay," O'Reilly said, nodding his head. This hadn't been what he thought Bev meant when she said his evening wasn't over yet. He should've known better than to be thinking with *that* head.

Beverly patted his knee for reassurance as footsteps approached. A large man with wild gray hair came around the corner carrying a tray of cups, saucers, and a teapot. He set it down on the coffee table and passed them out. His movements were slow to the point O'Reilly wanted to help him. When Bev gave him a look he quickly sat on his large hands.

"Oh, I forgot the scones," the man said, and turned to shuffle back into the kitchen.

Beverly spun on O'Reilly and wagged a finger in his face. "Behave." He was shocked by the flare of anger in her eyes.

The older man returned, set the plate of scones down on the table, and planted his bulk in a well-worn recliner.

He lifted his head and with a warm smile said, "Help yourselves; don't be shy." He poured tea for the three of them, and then took a scone for himself. Beverly plated a scone for O'Reilly but didn't take one for herself.

"So you brought me another unbeliever, did you, dear girl?" he chuckled and flecks of scone fell into his lap.

"Uncle Pete, I was telling Jim that you were an expert in the field of Spiritualism." She turned to O'Reilly and repeated what she had already told him in the car. "My uncle is a professor of religion at the University. I'm sure he'll be able to answer any of your questions."

O'Reilly stared at her with his mouth full then realized that was his cue to start talking. He chewed in a hurry and attempted to swallow the dry pastry but failed. He set the plate down and picked up the tea cup, taking a long drink to wash the lump down.

Wiping his mouth, he withdrew his notebook and glanced at his notes. "Ah yes, well, Mr.…"

"Call me Pete, Jim."

"All right, Pete, I have a strange case of a comatose young man in his late twenties talking in his sleep, as it were. The things he's saying are a bit disturbing. Bev thought you might be able to help me understand the significance, if any, of why or how this is happening."

Pete set his cup down. His eyes twinkled with delight that spread to his smile. "So my favorite niece has convinced you that the answer lies in the spirit world, has she? Oh, I know," he raised a hand to stop O'Reilly's objection. "You're a non-believer and she probably threatened you to come, am I right?" He winked at Bev, who blushed.

"Uncle Pete, you make me sound bad."

He laughed. "Now dear, I'm just having some fun with you." He looked at O'Reilly. "But I'm right, aren't I?"

O'Reilly couldn't help but laugh. He liked the old guy. "Oh, yeah."

"Well, let me see if I can at least give you some information." Pete's tone was more serious now. "It will be up to you to believe or not." He sat back and steepled his fingers. "Let me see, where to begin? A brief history would help, I suppose.

"The words spirit, soul, mind, psyche, and self are all synonymous, or at least they will be for the basis of this discussion. They all have similarities but many have associated terms or purposes for each.

"Plato believed the soul was the essence of a person. Thomas Aquinas taught that every organism had a soul, but only man's was immortal. The soul is connected more closely to spirituality and religion, whereas spirit seeks to rise above any of those entanglements.

"Spiritism or spiritualism is actually a system of beliefs based on the assumption that communicating with the dead or spirits is possible. Spiritualism is a religion that came into existence around the 1840s in upstate New York. They believe that spirits residing in the spirit world have both the ability and inclination to talk to the living. They postulate that the soul continues to exist after the loss of its physical shell, and even after death the soul can learn and improve."

He took a sip of his tea and frowned. "Cold. Spiritualists see the afterlife as a series of higher levels or planes, that can be attained through evolving. They don't believe that the short time a person spends on earth is the basis for assigning a soul to an eternity in heaven or hell. They are able to attain those levels in a constant progression."

"So to be clear here, we're talking about ghosts, right?" Jim's tone was clearly disbelieving.

Bev smacked Jim's leg. "You promised."

"Now, now, dear girl. Allow the man his opinion." To Jim, he said, "She's feisty but if you can get past that, she's really a good girl and worth the risk of an occasional minor injury."

"Uncle Pete!"

"Yeah, I can see that, although only time will tell about the risk being worth it." Jim said.

Beverly huffed, crossed her arms, and did not reply.

"Now sir, back to your question. Are we speaking of ghosts? I'm not sure, but I do not think so. Let me explain. Ghosts or apparitions seem to be tied to certain locations where their beings lived or suffered. They communicate by appearing or rattling things around a house, but they are never reported to have spoken. People who have reported seeing ghosts say they felt a chill first or sensed a presence.

Oh, occasionally people have claimed that a ghost has told them something that the person couldn't have known, or given some warning of impending doom, but they are never reliable or proven."

He took another bite of his scone.

"Ghosts have been with us for centuries. If so many have claimed to have seen them over the years, then it stands to reason that they must exist. No matter what religion or science says about the existence of ghosts, people continue to report paranormal experiences."

"But isn't that like believing that vampires are real?"

"Not really. See, there is no evidence that a supernatural being like a vampire ever existed. There is evidence that supports a murderous ruler who spiked heads, but the fiction grew from that. There have been reports of ghost sightings for so long that there has to be something to it."

"Okay, but how does that help me? Is this guy a medium who can speak with the dead?"

"It may not be necessary for him to be a channeller. You say he is in a coma, near death. He's probably able to touch the spirit world."

"So there's a ghost haunting the hospital? Is it important

to know who it might be?"

"If it's a ghost, then yes. There is a reason for that ghost to be tied to the hospital. Perhaps they died there and can't accept their loss. But have there been other reports of sightings? And from what you say, there was nothing visual; only audible. No, I'm more inclined to believe it's a spirit. Spirits are not tied to any one location. The spirit may have found a connection through this individual and is trying to send a warning. Spiritualism also believes there are spirit guides who can reach out to certain receptive humans. They can share knowledge of the afterlife. Obviously there is no proof."

O'Reilly folded his notepad and placed it back in his pocket. "So I'm really no closer to understanding this, ah, phenomenon."

Pete leaned forward. "Look, whether you believe in spirits or not, can you afford to treat this 'phenomenon', as you call it, as anything other than a real threat? What if whoever this is is really trying to warn you of an impending explosion in our city?" He sat back. "No; if I were you, I would heed the warning."

CHAPTER

Forty-Six

For a long spell, I sat and replayed the highlights of my nonexistent life, fighting hard to shake off the morose. The choice I made to stop the bombers cheated me of my happily-ever-after in the end. I sat pondering my fate for longer than intended.

There would be enough time to think about my loss later. I needed to check on O'Reilly and see if he made any progress with my clues.

Popping in at the police station, I searched the detectives' floor but he wasn't there. Where the hell was he? Didn't he understand the importance of what he was told? Impatience was making me angry. Time was running out. If O'Reilly didn't start now it would be too late to stop the bombers.

I began to pace, then I started to twirl. Faster and faster, my speed increased until I had become a mini ghostnado. When I stopped, it was into O'Reilly's chair. I started whirling in fast circles until I realized the chair wasn't spinning, it was just me.

What was he doing that was more important than saving lives? Then it came to me. It wasn't what he was doing, but who he was doing. I forgot. He was out on a date. There was no telling where he was or how long he would be there. Jumping in and out of scenes and threads and having no concept of passing time any more, the darkness had not registered with me. It was after midnight. O'Reilly wouldn't show up at the station again until the morning. If then.

Now what?

I decided to check on Mac and see if he'd recovered enough to go again. If O'Reilly wasn't going to act on Mac's message I would- er, Mac would have to keep trying to deliver the message. Hopefully someone would understand before it was too late.

Mac was sitting with his hands on the sides of his head, just staring forward. The only reason I knew he wasn't in some sort of trance was that his eyes blinked when I came into view.

"Mac, you okay, buddy?"

"Do I look okay? I'm in pain. I'm supposed to be in this coma to avoid the pain and to heal, but you keep causing me more pain and then I relapse instead of heal. I can't do it anymore. I want to help; I do, but I can't keep trying at the risk of losing my own life." He shifted his body and looked at me.

"I'm sorry. I know I said I'd do it, but you can't know how bad the pain is or the damage these returns are causing."

Closing my eyes, I pictured the man who had shot me. I saw how he strutted with arrogance and knew he was about to get away with mass murder—for profit. Opening my eyes, I sagged my shoulders in defeat. "Okay, Mac, I know you did the best you could. I don't want to hurt you. I just wish there was a way for me to take your place because I know I wouldn't quit until those people were safe."

I raised my hands in front of me as Mac began to protest. "Whoa! I'm not trying to be insulting. I'm merely stating the fact. I know how I am. For me to push my desires on you was wrong. I can't help how I am just like you can't help how you are."

"What's that supposed to mean?" Mac stood. "You saying I'm chicken or something? You think it's wrong for me not to go back because I value my life over others'?"

He was angry. I risked losing him for good. And in truth, maybe that was the best for him. At least he would have a chance to live.

"No, Mac, I think you're very brave."

"Bullshit!"

"I'm serious. I had no idea you would be hurt as bad as you were that first time. But even after knowing it would hurt horribly, you went back twice more. To me, that took a lot of guts. I won't ask you to go back again, although your family is poised around your bed waiting for your return." That was mostly speculation but probably not far off.

"You've done enough." I stuck out my hand. "I'm proud of you and want to thank you for trying." Mac stared at my outstretched hand. "I know what you're doing. You're hoping to guilt me into going back by saying it's all right to quit. I know that's what you're doing, but it's not going to work, man. I'm going to stay here until my body calls me back. So take your guilt and disappear."

I looked from Mac to my hand then lowered it.

"Bye, Mac. I hope you have a great life."

"Wa-wait! You're actually going?"

"Yeah, isn't that what you wanted?"

"Well yeah, but I thought you were so gung-ho about saving those people. What happened?"

"I listened to you and realized you were right. It wasn't fair of me to sacrifice your future to save others. You deserve a future with Caroline. So enjoy. Name one of your kids after me."

I started to go again.

"That's it? You're just giving up?"

"Yes. Now let me go."

"What if I tried once more? Okay? Just once more, then we're done."

The shock on his face was greater than that on mine. *I can't believe I said that!* was written all over his face. I tried to hide my smile. I could tell he was trying to think of a way to take back the words.

"Ah, well, if that's what you want. It's totally up to you. Is that what you want to do?"

"No, it's not what I want to do, but I guess since I said it, I'll go back once more. But only once more. You understand?"

"I understand."

"How the hell did you do that?"

I laughed. "Hey buddy, that was all you."

"Whatever."

He frowned and looked around his space as if searching for a way to escape. I didn't blame him. I understood exactly how he felt.

"Do me one favor?" he asked. "Go see if they upped the drugs."

"Sure."

The scene in the room was pretty much as I expected it to be. The chairs had been pulled up close to the bed. The usual three still held their vigil. Hope had bloomed new tension. It showed on their faces and in the tightness of their raised and bunched shoulders. They were exhausted yet refused to give in to sleep's call.

A night shift nurse entered. "Any change?"

"No," Mrs. MacIntosh's voice was a whisper.

"You should take turns watching him so each of you can

get some rest. You are so stressed out, you're all on the verge of exhaustion. Really; one can watch and call for the others if anything changes. I can get you some blankets and you can crash in the waiting room."

No one responded. They all continued to watch Mac as if afraid they might miss something. It was like being on a whale watching tour and being in the bathroom the only time a whale broke the surface. They didn't want to budge.

The nurse gave a knowing smile. "I'm giving him his next dose of pain meds. The doctor okayed the continued increase once more after this, and then he said he would cut it by half to keep your son safe."

"Thank you," Caroline said.

"Try to get some rest," the nurse said, then left the room.

Mac was doing some deep breathing exercises when I returned. It was obviously only for his mental state but I understood his reasoning.

"Okay Mac, they just gave you a fresh dose. The nurse said there would only be one more after this. We have to make something happen this time. You're going to need to rest after that because when the next dose runs out the amount will be cut in half. One way or the other we both have less than a day left."

CHAPTER

Forty-Seven

Mac's first word, 'bomb', caused all three watchers to jump and squeal. Caroline tossed the pen she held in the air and had to drop to the floor to retrieve it. She scribbled furiously, trying to sneak peeks at her boyfriend between the tears and her jotting.

"Tomorrow. Bomb. Cop killed. Chance. Bomb. Dead. Bomb. Many. Help. Police. Hurts. Love. You. Bom…"

"Oh Garrett, please come back." Caroline dropped the pen and paper and threw herself on the bed and sobbed. "Please. I can't take it anymore." She draped her arms over Mac's body. His mother came over and gently lifted the distraught woman from her son. She turned Caroline to face her and gave her a big motherly hug, rubbing her back in a comforting way. Barney looked shaken and emotionally drained as well. This time he never left the room to retrieve the nurse.

We both saw the tear at the same time. Barney walked to the bed and reached through the bandages and gently wiped his son's face. I had to wipe away my own tears. Watching the scene before me, I knew then that I wouldn't ask Mac to try again. His family could not take the torment any longer. I was teasing them with their son's life. I felt every bit the monster I was.

As I left the hospital room, Barney huddled up to the two women, embracing them protectively. He looked toward the ceiling and I knew he was asking God for the help he deserved.

Back in Mac's brain, I found him sitting where he was before in the same position. The difference was that this time, his body was shaking uncontrollably. The pain had to have been severe, yet my goading had made him stay longer than he should have. Now he was paying the price for my insults.

"I'm sorry, Mac. You did real well. You *are* the bravest man I've ever known. You did what you said you would. Now I'm going to keep my word too. I won't be coming back. Whatever happens now, we—you—did your best to prevent the catastrophe from happening. Goodbye."

I shot skyward to my perch. In seconds I was on a baseball field, running bases as fast as I could. A few hundred laps later I stopped. The one good thing about being dead was I no longer needed to sleep. The blessing there was I would not be having the nightmares that would have plagued me when I was alive.

I should've watched to see what Caroline did with her notes, but somehow it didn't matter anymore. Controlling the outcome on earth was beyond my capabilities. I wasn't God, but I did wonder if He was so all powerful, how come He didn't step in to prevent some of these man-made catastrophes from occurring? If I was so worked up about the death and destruction, how could He just sit back and watch without lifting a finger to help? That didn't seem too Godlike to me.

While the events of the past few days ran like a never ending NASCAR race through my head, I conjured up a pitching machine, batting cage, helmet, and bat. Then I proceeded to take out my aggressions on the baseballs.

I cranked the speed up to a hundred and twenty miles an

hour and was still cracking the ball pretty good. What an amazing feeling! If I could've done that when I was alive, I'd still be playing. The pitches came faster and the blasts off my bat went farther.

Without being aware of the change, my joyful smile morphed into an angry hateful mask. I was no longer trying to hit the ball. Instead I was trying to crush it, not caring how far the ball went, but more interested in tearing the cover off it.

Then through the red haze of my rage, a single thought began to form until it was beaming like a light through the darkness. The next pitch shattered my bat, leaving splinters in my hands. I stared at the remains. *"Damn! I still don't know where the bomb is."*

CHAPTER

Forty-Eight

In an instant, the field was gone. I was standing on my cloud looking down, my eyes moving from point to point to point, not knowing where to go. I may not be able to affect the outcome but I had to see where all Mac's and my efforts led.

Mac was out. I promised him. That left finding O'Reilly or Hipsher.

I jumped to the station. The clock showed it was after seven in the morning. The detectives' floor was coming to life; however, there was no sign of O'Reilly. My nerves were firing on full automatic.

I circled his desk for half an hour then decided to go find Hipsher. Regardless what O'Reilly did, I still had to find the location of the bomb and get it to him, or our efforts would be all for naught.

Blinking to Hipsher's place, I searched his rooms. He was gone. Looking closer, I noticed there were more things missing than I'd seen him pack. The refrigerator was almost empty, his closet seemed rather sparse, and there appeared to be a few blank spaces on shelves and walls where pictures might have been.

The bathroom, however, still had some of the obvious things you might expect to find; as though Hipsher had packed but wanted anyone checking to think he was still around. I had lost him. I needed to flash back to the last place I saw him in order to find him again, but that would waste precious time.

I caught up to Hipsher the night before when he was coming home. I watched him pack some more things and go to bed. Very early the next day he rose and loaded his car. It was still dark. The last time I saw him he was on the expressway leaving town. He wasn't going to lead me to the bomb. He was a dead end. Either someone else was placing the bomb or it was already on site. I would have to leave Hipsher for later.

Now I was at a loss as to how to find the bomb. If Hipsher never went near it, how could I find it? I had to think. In the meantime, I zapped back to the precinct. O'Reilly was just entering. It was half past eight. He was humming, which must have meant things went well with Nurse Bev.

He sat at his desk and began looking through messages, whistling as he read them. Detective Pollen walked by and stopped.

"Uh-oh, somebody got lucky last night."

O'Reilly's face reddened. "Pollen, shush!" He glanced around the room embarrassed. A few of the other detectives began riding him.

Pollen sat on the edge of the desk. In a quieter voice he said, "So things went well with your friend, I take it?"

O'Reilly blushed again. "Ah, yeah, you could say that. It started out nice then turned really weird before ending up with a bang, if you know what I mean."

"You dog. What was the weird part?"

O'Reilly stopped at one message and smiled. "In fact, she already called." He reached for the phone on his desk. "I'll tell you later. Take a walk for a minute, would ya?"

"No problem. Who'd want to hear you get all lovey-dovey anyway? Maybe you'll get dinner and dessert again tonight."

Pollen moved to his desk as O'Reilly made his call.

"Hey, Bev. How you doing this morning?" If he expected Bev to say what a great time she'd had last night and could they do it again, he was very wrong.

"Jim, you have to get over here right now!"

O'Reilly became alert with concern.

"Why? What happened?"

"That boy spoke again. His fiancée wrote down his words."

"Oh, ah, well, that kinda sounds more like something for the doctor to check out to me."

"Jim O'Reilly, we had a deal. You got what you wanted and now it's my turn."

O'Reilly was flabbergasted. "You mean you only did that so I would investigate something a comatose boy said?"

There was silence on the line. When Beverly spoke again her voice was much calmer. "No, Jim, that's not why. To tell you the truth, I'm not sure why I let things go that far. I've been thinking about it all morning. That's not like me at all. It usually takes a long time before I allow someone to get that close to me, especially physically. I-I don't know what to say about that, except I'm embarrassed."

"Oh, I'm sorry you feel that way. We didn't have to do anything at all. I was happy just being with you. I hope what happened doesn't change anything between us. I'd really like to see you again. And honest; nothing has to happen."

"I'm happy to hear that. Let me think about it. I did have a good time, but I'm serious about this boy. There is something going on here. Someone is trying to communicate from the other side and it sounds important."

"I don't know what you expect me to do about it, Bev.

I'm sorry, but I just don't believe in that stuff."

"Look, Jim, I'm not asking you to believe in the spirit world. I'm asking you to believe in me. Sometimes strange things happen for unexplained reasons. Look at us. What are the chances that out of the blue I would call you? You couldn't possibly have known that you would've ended up in my bed last night, but you did. I never, ever, am that easy, yet there I was.

Perhaps something put us together for a reason. If you wouldn't have believed any of that could've happened and it did, maybe, just maybe, something even stranger could happen too."

Huh! Suddenly I had a strange feeling come over me. It *was* kinda coincidental. My thoughts raced for a solution. The only answer came back as Les. Would he have done that? Could he do that? Nah, he wouldn't make Bev sleep with the detective, especially not to help me. There had to be a canon of ghostly ethics that forbid that sort of thing.

"Sometimes it takes a leap of faith to find the answer. I'm asking, with no strings or promises, that you at least check it out. What could it hurt? And by that same miracle that caused you to end up in my bed, perhaps you might discover a terrorist plot to blow something up and become a hero."

"Wow! That was some speech. Look, Bev, no promises, but I'll check into it, all right? But instead of me coming down there, why don't you read me what he said. If he speaks again, call me, but make sure you write it down too."

"Thanks, Jim. I really appreciate this. Oh, and why don't we meet later for dinner and—whatever?"

O'Reilly's smile wrapped around his face. "Sounds like a plan. I'll call you. Now what were those words?"

CHAPTER

Forty-Nine

I watched over his shoulder as O'Reilly jotted down Mac's words as Bev read them to him. He stared at them for a moment before pulling out his notebook. He compared the two lists.

Bomb-tomorrow-hurts-cop-swift-killed-Al-bomb-help-hurts

Tomorrow-bomb-cop killed-Chance-bomb-dead-bomb-many-help-police-hurts-love-you-bomb

He was still studying the lists minutes later when Pollen again perched on the corner of the desk.

"What's got you so puzzled, big man? Didn't the phone call from your friend go well? You didn't get dumped already, did you?"

"She's got me working some riddle."

"Uh-oh, she's already got you working for her?"

"It's nothing I've ever dealt with before. I don't have a clue as to how to handle this. I don't want to let Bev down, but I'm out of my element here."

"Is this the weird thing you were telling me about?"

"Yeah." He looked up from the list and said, "Do you believe that people can communicate with the dead?"

"Oh no. She's not a creature feature, is she?"

O'Reilly laughed. "A what?"

"You know, someone who believes in ghosts and vampires and alien beings."

O'Reilly raised an eyebrow. "Yeah, I think she might be.

I spent an interesting evening with her uncle learning about spiritualism. It's some far out stuff. However, I actually did hear this kid talk."

"It wasn't a séance, was it?"

"No; nothing like that. There's this kid in the hospital that was in a motorcycle accident. He's in a coma. Doctor says he's lucky to be alive. In fact, my friend said the doctor thought he was so badly hurt that keeping him alive might be a waste of time and had broached the subject about pulling the plug with the family before he started speaking.

"Anyway, the kid isn't awake, but suddenly he starts spouting off about a bomb. I was there and heard him. But he never regained consciousness. It was just this eerie voice coming out of this bandaged up face. Definitely weird."

I began to get excited.

"Now, I'm thinking he's dreaming about something. You know, like he was in this crash and maybe to his mind it was like an explosion or like a bomb went off."

Pollen said, "Or it could be that he was building a bomb when the accident occurred."

O'Reilly frowned, "Yeah, sure; give credence to this. Thanks."

"Hey, just saying. I'm just glad it's your puzzle and not mine."

"You're a big help."

This was too frustrating. If only they could see what I saw.

"You know you're gonna have to go through the motions if you ever want to get back in her pants again."

Absently O'Reilly said, "Yeah, that's what I'm thinking."

"Huh! So you did get lucky last night?" Pollen said way

too loud.

All eyes turned toward O'Reilly. Some made comments; some applauded.

"Bastard!" He said to Pollen, who laughed. "Oh, go back to work!" O'Reilly yelled to the others.

Pollen stood up to leave. "Yeah, run away, you prick," O'Reilly said.

"So, check out the kid and report back to your friend. It's easy. Did he say anything else?"

"Yeah, stuff like 'tomorrow,' which I guess now means today. 'Killed' and 'cop.'"

"He killed a cop?"

"I'm not sure that's what he means. Maybe a cop gets killed by the bomb."

O'Reilly had Pollen's attention now. He put his hands on the desk and leaned forward. "What else?"

"Ah, let's see. He says 'dead' and 'police.'"

"That's no help, but there is a theme."

I began rooting out loud. It was like being given word clues on a game show and trying to blurt out the answer.

"Well, then he says, 'swift.' Not sure what that means except maybe happens fast."

"Huh! Is that it?"

"He says a name, 'Chance." He also said, 'Al.'"

"That could be El, as in someone Arabic speaking. Perhaps it's the name of the bomber."

My hope faded. I screamed my frustration for all the good that did.

O'Reilly said, "Alleged bomber."

Pollen stood and turned to leave. "Well, good luck with that. If I were you I'd check out this guy real good just in case he's making swift bombs with this Chance character."

"Thanks for the support."

Pollen waved over his shoulder as he was walking away. He reached his desk and stood over a pile of folders. Then, as if someone strapped a board to his body, he stiffened. A curious look came over his face and he began rubbing the back of his neck.

He turned and faced O'Reilly. "Wait. Swift? Chance? Chance Swift?" He put a hand on his chin and massaged it like he was thinking. "Oh, this is too weird." I froze and held my breath. Pollen rummaged through his files. Finding the one he wanted, he flipped through the contents, knowing what they said before he read them. He paused staring at the name then hurried back to O'Reilly.

"Son of a bitch, look at this—Chance Swift. He's that unsolved case I was telling you about the other day. He was found shot to death in an alley about three days ago. I haven't made much headway on it. I'm still waiting for lab results on blood we found on the scene and I only just found out his address."

The two men looked at each other, and then Pollen started lyrically with, "Doo-doo-doo-doo-doo-doo-doo-doo. This is real *Twilight Zone* stuff."

"Sounds more like a lot of doo-doo to me."

"Well, you do have to admit, it's kinda spooky."

"No," O'Reilly said, shaking his head. He stood up. "I am not going to believe that this Chance Swift is trying to talk to us from beyond the grave. No way, no how. It can't be true." He caught Pollen's eye. "Can it?"

Yes! I pumped my arm like I had just homered off Nolan Ryan.

CHAPTER

Fifty

"Okay, let's get a grip on reality here," said Pollen. "I may not believe in ghosts, but I believe less in coincidences."

"What are you saying? That we should treat the bomb as if it's a real threat?"

"I don't think we can take a chance that it's not."

O'Reilly looked around nervously. "Do we tell someone?"

Pollen caught what O'Reilly was saying. They could be laughed off the force if they mentioned what they were thinking and it turned out to be nothing.

"No, not yet. Let's do legwork first. You check out your kid. I'll look deeper into Swift. We have to find out if there is any connection between them. Also, find out if they have any ties to terrorist groups, militia units, or any other nutcase groups on any sort of watch list."

"We have to hurry. If this is real, that bomb will go off sometime today."

"Shit!"

* * *

While the two men worked feverishly on their computers researching Mac and me, I fled the scene. Now it was more imperative than ever that I find that bomb.

I already knew that Hipsher was gone. He would be no

help locating the bomb. My other options were to go back to my death and follow the three assailants. One or all of them would lead me to the bomb.

Picturing the scene, I hopped straight there. I picked a moment after my death so I wouldn't have to relive it yet again. The three men staggered from the alley and I followed. They got into a car and drove. Twenty minutes later, they stopped in a Wal-Mart parking lot. Two of the men got out and climbed into different cars. When they left the parking lot, it was in three separate directions. I had to make a choice and hoped I got it right.

I followed the man who I saw in the alley the night I met Monica. I had a clear mental picture of him standing there with his lowlife friends, watching Monica and me walk by. I remember seeing myself eyeball him and the way he glared back at me. I had prepared for battle should he and his friends try something.

The car drove for quite a while before stopping at a pharmacy. He purchased things to clean his cuts and pills to ease his pain. I hoped he hurt all night long.

He got back in his car, popped the lid off the pain pills and swallowed four of them. He looked at himself in the rearview mirror. With one hand he pulled back his lip and examined the cut and his loose teeth and the hole where the missing one had been. He should feel lucky I didn't knock them all down his throat. He started the car and drove off.

I thought back and remembered the punch that hit his mouth. A tooth had cut one of my knuckles. I glanced at my hand now and saw the cut appear. As I stared at it, a strange sensation passed through me.

Wait a minute; something was wrong here. I was going about this the wrong way. I hadn't thought it through yet. I slid through the roof of the car and sat in the back seat.

I was missing a chunk of this story and before I went any further I had to think.

In the version that could've been, I beat up the bad guys but left them in the alley, right? But there would've been a cut or at least a scab where the tooth had torn into me. How was it I was on that street and chose that diner to meet Monica? And why hadn't I heard anything about a bomb either being defused or exploding?

Then it came to me like a slap in the face. I was following the wrong thread. In the thread where I met Monica, I hadn't gotten involved with the terrorists. So the bombs should've gone off. What happened?

Damn! I was going to have to start all over.

CHAPTER

Fifty-One

I had to hurry. Just because I could move through decades in a blink of an eye, real time still passed by in seconds and they were ticking away. When I had watched my future with Monica, I skipped ahead to the highlights. I didn't follow day to day life. I stopped at all the important places that had to do with Monica or our family. I skimmed over the boring.

This time I slowed the thread down. I went back to that first night I met Monica. When I left her at her apartment building, it was only eight o'clock. I was on such a euphoric high I jumped straight from that moment to the next time we saw each other. I didn't stop to listen to our conversation; I just continued to move forward, basking in Monica's radiance.

This time though, wanting to see more of what happened that night, but still being aware of real time, I made jumps forward in fifteen minute increments.

Five jumps later it happened: a deep rumble in the distance, followed by a huge ball of flame that lit the night sky. I felt the initial blast as the ground shook and again moments later as the concussion washed over me. The bomb had gone off. How could I have not known?

My only excuse was that I was so enraptured by Monica that I hadn't paid attention to the world around us. Surely the explosion would have been the topic of conversation, but I skipped ahead so far in our budding relationship that world events didn't register.

I stood, mouth agape, at the sight and the implications. Then, before I realized, the real me was running toward the blast site. It was at least a mile away but I never slowed down until I was in the midst of the chaos, the insanity, and the death.

I lowered into my old physical body to witness the destruction from a person's point of view. The screams filled my head. In this alternate reality, I ran into the carnage and began helping whoever I could. Guilt covered me along with the blood of the wounded and dying. After all the fighting and death I had been a part of in Afghanistan, nothing could have prepared me for the devastation and loss of life I now observed. Shock and horror assaulted my senses at every turn.

The agony was palpable. Blood and body parts were strewn and mingled. The smell of seared flesh rose from the ground like smoke. The endless carnage stretched out before me like a medieval battle ground. The scene was overwhelming.

This thread was what would have been if I never took the flash drive. That's why there was no recognition when I saw my attacker in that alley. With a saddened and aching heart, I erased the memory of this thread and went back to find where I had gone wrong.

Retracing the thread of my death, I stopped back in the alley just before the confrontation. Freezing the scene, I studied the players. I was missing something. There were no other alternatives from this point other than my death. Any options that could've altered the outcome happened between when I stole the flash drive and this point. I went back further.

There I was, taking the flash drive and running. As I increased the distance between myself and the two men, three new paths illuminated before me. I did the freeze frame thing again and tried to remember what I was thinking. Here was where I made the choice that led to my death.

I ran home and loaded the flash drive to my computer. I needed to make a copy before I turned it over to the police. I wanted to make sure the contents were legit. If I ran into the police station with some film student's final movie project, I'd look like the world's biggest fool.

That was my reasoning for going home first. It was sound and I still would do it. How could I know the bad guys had a cop who could track me down?

The menu had three parts. I opened the schematics and the display showed a very large bomb. There was no information as to what kind of explosive device it was or how big. It could've been dirty. The two series of numbers could've been arming and disarming codes. There was nothing that confirmed the bomb was real and set to go off. It could just be a game but I couldn't take the chance.

Deciding to risk embarrassment, I downloaded all three files, but never opened the file that detailed where the bomb was located and where it would be detonated. I was in too much of a hurry to get the information into the hands of the police.

That was the end of the story and ultimately of me. They found me a few blocks from my apartment building. I ducked into the alley and the rest is history now.

I zipped back to my other options.

Following the second thread led me to the police station. I pushed through the doors, my eyes sweeping the lobby. Finding the front desk I headed straight for it when I felt a hand wrap around my arm. I spun, ready to throw fists until I realized it wasn't one of the bombers. However, I recognized the man even if my real me didn't. It was Hipsher.

The bombers would have called him. He probably stationed himself there, waiting in case I showed up at the station.

"Can I help you, sir? You seem to be agitated about something."

"I have information about a bombing here in the city. I need to get it to someone who can stop it."

"A bombing? Really? Come with me. I can help you."

Hearing him now, I should've been suspicious by his lack of reaction. I followed him through a side door, along a hallway, through a large room full of desks and cops, and into an interrogation room. He had me sit.

"Now, why don't you tell me about this bomb?"

I laid it out for him and handed over the flash drive. He told me to sit tight while he did some checking. Ten minutes later, an officer came for me and led me down to the basement where he put me into a cell.

I skipped ahead. I was questioned as if I were the bomber. When I mentioned the flash drive, Hipsher denied ever seeing it. I could already see where this was heading. When the bomb went off I would be the prime suspect. This thread was going nowhere fast. I leaped back to the final thread.

CHAPTER

Fifty-Two

Being a suspect in several assaults and therefore having a natural fear of cops, I stopped in the lobby of a high-rise office building and phoned a friend.

"Joe, it's me. Hey, I gotta a major problem and need your help." Pause. "Nah; not on the phone. Besides, I have to give you something. This is really important. Drop everything and meet me now. You know where. Fifteen minutes. I'm counting on you, man; don't let me down."

Joe was ten minutes late. Each minute that passed made me want to strangle him to the point I almost leapt for his throat when he arrived.

"Chill, man! Stop looking at me like you want to hurt me. What's so damn important anyway?"

I took a deep breath and looked Joe over for any tell-tale signs he was using again. He was a slender, young black man who had gotten into trouble with a drug dealer. Joe was selling and became his own best customer. When he didn't have the money his boss demanded, his life was forfeit.

Through another client I had helped, Joe's mother and sister contacted me, asking for assistance. They had nothing to pay me with, but I took the case anyway. I was too emotional to be much of a businessman. When someone was in trouble I usually helped, regardless of payment. My lack of funds was a testament to that practice.

I was able to step in and make Joe's debt go away. The fact that the drug dealer disappeared didn't hurt Joe's situation either. After long months of rehab at my expense, Joe was back in the world and trying to function. It had been about six months now. I prayed he had been able to stay clean.

He seemed a little too edgy. That worried me.

"You using?"

"What? No, man …"

"Look at me. If you're using again you tell me right now. This is too important for me to trust it to some worthless junkie. Too many lives may be at stake."

"Hey," Joe was angry. "Don't you call me that. I don't care who you are or what you did for me, you don't call me that. I ain't using."

"Then why you acting strung out?"

"It's you, man. You scare the shit out of me. I heard the rumors about what happened to De La Rosa. I don't want that happening to me. You call me and say we have to meet and I get, you know, a little nervous about what your intent is."

"You stay clean and you never have to worry about me coming after you. You've stayed clean, right?"

Joe glanced down. "Yeah, I'm clean. I swear." Then he looked at me. "But I still think about it. It scares me. I don't want to drug up again, but it's like an evil spirit, always calling me. When will it stop calling to me?"

I put a hand on Joe's shoulder. It was meant to be comforting, but I felt the flinch. "It may never stop trying to drag you down again, but it's grip will get weaker in time. Every day that passes, the drug loses some of its hold on you. After all you've gone through, don't give in to its call. It would be just like putting a gun to your head. I've got too much invested in you for you to quit on me. You're a very strong man. You can do this. Think about how proud your mother and sister are of you."

I dropped my hand and backed up a step. What I was about to say next might cause a reaction. "You know, your sister was so desperate for me to help you that she offered herself to me as payment."

Joe's head shot up. A spark of rage flashed in his eyes.

"If she was willing to give her body to save you, don't you think she deserves the same commitment from you?"

"She—you—tell me…"

"Joe, you should know me better than that. I never touched your sister."

I never planned on telling him that, but I needed him focused. I think the revelation had the desired effect. Joe relaxed. His eyes went watery.

"But don't you dare mention this to her. It would hurt her if you knew what she was willing to do to help save you. Promise me."

He nodded and wiped his eyes.

"So what's so important?"

I showed him the flash drive. "It's time for you to pay me back and become a hero. The information on this flash drive will save thousands of lives. You need to get this to the police right now. No delays. For reasons best left unsaid, I can't do it. Keep my name out of it if you can."

"Okay, but what should I say?"

"Tell them someone paid you to bring the flash drive and it involves a bomb. You can do this. It's important."

Joe took the flash drive and stared at it. "Joe, a lot of lives are depending on you. Put it in your pocket."

He nodded and did as I said.

"You're a good man, Joe. Stay strong."

I shook his hand and he left.

CHAPTER

Fifty-Three

So there was a chance that in one of the threads I was able to stop the blast. I wanted to jump ahead and see if I still met Monica, but as much as I wanted to know if we still had a future, time was too short in reality. I had to discover where the bomb was and get the information to the police.

This time, when I rushed into the blast site, I concentrated more on the details of the site, blocking the writhing masses within the carnage below from my mind. I was in River View Park in the downtown area of the city. The large grass covered plot, as its name indicated, ran along the banks of the river. The remains of a stage burned at the far end of where I hovered. Bits of debris smoked in spiraling black columns on the water. There must have been a concert going on. So, now that I knew where the bomb was going to be, I needed to find where it was before it reached that location.

If the bomber was close and saw the police or bomb sniffing dogs searching for it, they could detonate the bomb by remote. The safest solution would be to find the device before it could be placed on site. I still needed to follow one of my attackers. In an instant I was in the back seat of the car with Toothless Man.

Our journey ended when he pulled into a parking lot of a music store. I thought, Great! The bomber was an out of work musician. He parked behind the building and used a key to enter the business from the rear. He stepped into a large warehouse stocked with massive speakers, soundboards, thousands of feet of cables, lights, racks, and everything you could imagine for DJs or bands to use.

Toothless, as I now referred to him, walked past the entire inventory and through a door that led to the store front. Behind a counter stood another man who was helping a customer create his own unique sound system.

Toothless nodded and went to a computer on the counter. He typed a bit and then studied what was on the screen. He pushed a button and the printer started. Reaching under the counter, he retrieved a sheet of paper and read it.

"I'm gonna start loading the equipment for the show tonight," he said.

The other man nodded.

Back in the storage room, he began assembling the items listed on the paper. The amount of equipment needed suggested that whatever the event they were doing must be big. And since it was in River View Park, it was huge. By my estimation, the park's area could easily hold two hundred thousand people.

I floated around, searching the building for anything that looked like the diagram I'd seen on the flash drive. Nothing came close, but I couldn't see inside things. When he finished compiling equipment from the list, he lifted an overhead door and walked out. Watching him from the open doorway, I continued my search.

A few minutes later a truck backed into the warehouse, stopping fifteen feet from the collection of sound equipment. Toothless jumped down from the cab and walked to the rear. Lowering the hydraulic gate, he rode the lift up and opened the sliding door. Inside was a large equipment cabinet that looked like a trunk on heavy casters; the kind musicians used to load their miscellaneous gear.

My heart rate accelerated, or at least it felt like it did. I had to get a look inside that box, but how? I was so desperate the Jedi mind trick even came to mind. *What the heck.* "You will open the box. You will open the box. Open the box you will." Nothing. What did I really expect?

Toothless began loading the rest of the equipment around the box. When he was halfway done he scooted to the back of the truck, crouched down, and inserted a key into the trunk. I rushed to his side and bent low.

The hairs on the back of his neck rose before he turned and looked around the truck. While he was being paranoid I moved closer to the crack. *Lift it higher.* But the man was too spooked. Maybe he actually felt me get next to him.

He glanced back at the box as if debating whether to open it further. To be sure of what was in there, I needed him to raise it another six inches. I wished I could goose him.

He lowered the lid and I feared he would lock it, but instead he walked to the end of the truck and stood on the gate. His eyes swept the warehouse. He leaned around both sides of the truck and looked. His fears calmed and he came back to the crate and lifted the lid. The bomb was inside. He flipped up the lid of a small box attached to the top of the bomb and flicked a switch. Lights in the box came to life.

Taking a phone from his pocket, he made a call. "It's me. When are you coming?" I couldn't hear the reply. "But you said you were coming to arm the ..."

"Of course, I'm alone."

I squeezed between his ear and the phone. That would have made a good cartoon picture. A voice in the speaker said, "Relax, you can do this without me. I'll talk you through it."

The voice on the other end sounded like Hipsher. This guy obviously didn't know the cop had already skipped town. The bomber blew out a long breath. “What do I do?”

“Make sure the switch is off.”

The bomber leaned inside the crate and flicked the switch. The lights went off. “Okay.”

“Now lift the second lid. The one underneath where you found the switch.”

He fumbled to find the seam and without warning the lower lid popped open, causing him to jump back. He was sweating and I envisioned the drops were soaking me. “Okay. It is open.”

“Great! See? I told you it would be easy.”

“You also told me you would be here.”

Hipsher laughed. “Ah, plans do change, my friend. You're still getting what you want. Now, you see that long row of numbers?”

“Yes, they are all zeroes.”

Move each one to the number I tell you starting from left to right.” Hipsher recited the numbers and the bomber set each one.

“Now close the lid, switch the power on, and push that green button. The countdown will begin.”

The bomber did as instructed but his hand wavered over the green button. He must have speculated about the possibility Hipsher would double-cross him.

“Hello? You still there?”

“What will happen when I push the green button?”

Hipsher chuckled again. “What are you afraid of? That the bomb will go BOOM?” he shouted.

The bomber jumped as Hipsher had intended.

“Don't worry, my friend. I would not trick you. I won't

get the remainder of my money if the bomb goes off prematurely. The green button arms the bomb so that without the code number no one can disarm it. We good now?"

The black-haired man mumbled a prayer, closed his eyes, and pushed the button. He grimaced, preparing himself for the potential blast. Nothing happened. He opened one eye at a time, sighed and said, "Yes, we are good."

"All right. Good luck." Hipsher disconnected.

The sweating, toothless man closed the lid and then locked the crate. Now I knew where the bomb was and where it was going. I wasn't sure how long it would still be here, so even though I again promised to leave Mac alone, I had to get back to him fast.

I flew out the front window and stopped to read the name of the business. A large hand-painted sign hung above the front door. The bright white letters BSS were highlighted in red. Beneath them the words Big Sound Systems were printed in black. The address read 28451 Acadia St.

It was early afternoon. The blast would occur around nine thirty tonight; only seven- and-a-half hours remained to prevent the scene that would scar my dreams for eternity. Providing I slept, of course.

CHAPTER

Fifty-Four

For some reason, it was difficult getting back inside Mac's brain. I figured it was because of my haste. I tried several times and began to fear Mac had found a way to lock me out. With as much energy as I could create, I found a small crack in Mac's wall to slide through and entered an erotic dream about Caroline.

Mac was asleep, and in spite of his dream's subject matter, he looked very peaceful. I was glad to see he was getting the rest he needed. Too bad I was gonna have to wake him and send him back into the world of pain. I was hoping this would be the last time, even though I'd already promised he was done.

I leaned close, put a gentle hand on his shoulder and shook him, whispering, "Mac. Wake up. There's work to be done."

Mac's eyes opened slowly. When the sleep cleared from his vision he recognized me and smiled. It was a really big smile, which worried me.

"Hey, Chance, how's it going?" he yawned and stretched.

His eyes looked glazed and his words were slurred. If I didn't know better I'd think he was drunk. But there was no way he could get alcohol here. And the hospital certainly wouldn't slip any into his IV. *So what the heck was going on?*

Then it came to me. They must have increased his meds

again, thinking he was too much in pain to regain consciousness. The opposite had happened, however. Now Mac was too medicated, making him drowsy and lethargic.

Why now, when I was so close?

"Come on, Mac. Wake up."

I smacked his cheek lightly. Then I smacked it again, not so lightly. His reactions were slow. Wrapping my arms around him, I muscled Mac to his feet. His legs were rubbery and seemed to go all directions at once.

"Come on, Mac, walk." I started dragging him around his brain space.

"Man, Chance, I feel good. This is fun."

"Mac, move. Come on, try walking with me. I need you alert for this. I found the bomb. I know where it is and where it's gonna be. We can stop it but I need your help."

Mac's legs pretended to work, but I was the one supplying the power. I paced him back and forth vigorously. I bounced him, smacked him, yelled at him and ran with him, but none of my efforts were successful. Mac was zoned on pain meds. I could do nothing until they wore off enough for him to become coherent.

I set Mac down not very gently and jumped to the police station.

Pollen was just entering the room. O'Reilly was on the phone taking notes from whoever was on the other end. Pollen stopped at O'Reilly's desk and paced until the call was done. O'Reilly wrote a few more lines before looking up.

"Whatcha got, Jim?"

"There is absolutely no connection between the two men that I can find other than they're men who live in the same city."

"I drew a blank, too, although I think I have a lead on where Swift was staying. Why were you writing so much if you had nothing?"

"Uh, well, with nothing else to do, I called a psychic friend of Beverly's."

"A psychic? Seriously?"

"Hey, I had nothing else; I thought it couldn't hurt."

There was an awkward silence before Pollen said, "So what did she say?"

"What makes you think it's a woman?"

"Aren't all psychics?"

"Not this time. Dr. Ross Gilbert has more degrees than a thermometer. He totally believes in life after death and the ability to contact the dead---the other side, as he puts it. He's studied these occurrences for twenty years and says he has all the proof we would need to become believers if we're brave enough to visit him."

"And did this walking thermometer shed any light on the subject?"

"Other than being adamant that talking with the dead is not as rare as you think, no. He wants the name of the medium so he can study the phenomenon."

"You didn't give the name, did you?"

O'Reilly frowned. "Please, I'm not some rookie here."

"So do we need to go see this guy?"

"God, I hope not. We might not get out of there before tomorrow. What about you? Anything?"

"I was like you. I ran out of leads so I checked with the Feds to see if there was any terrorist alert they were keeping a lid on. I got nothing but a lot of questions. I hung up on the agent so I expect the Feds will be showing up here soon. I don't want to get caught here answering questions and wasting whatever time we have left. Let's head to the hospital so I can meet your ghost whisperer. Then we can make a stop at Swift's apartment to check it out."

O'Reilly cleared his throat. "Don't you think maybe it's time to let the Feds know what might be happening, or at least our own brass?"

"I don't know. On one hand, we've got nothing solid to go on except the words of a guy in a coma."

"Yeah, but if it is a real threat and that bomb goes off before we tell anyone, our careers are over. If not the FBI, then we should give a heads-up to someone here."

"Aw, man! Even if we tell the Feds they're never going to believe us. The guys here will laugh us out of town. Let's go see this Garrett and decide what to do after that. We need to hurry. If the bomb exists, we have no idea how much time we have."

CHAPTER

Fifty-Five

I was anxious now. The police were coming. I had to get Mac ready. When I arrived he was sitting up with a big silly smile on his face. “Hi, Chance. How’s it hanging in ghost world?”

“It’s not going so well, Mac. I need your help again.”

“You always need my help.”

“I know; I know. But listen. The cops are on their way here to listen to you. They don't believe what you’re saying. There’s only about six hours left before the bomb explodes. I’ve seen the damage it’s going to cause. It’s catastrophic. Mac, you have to go back. I have all the information you need to relay. Can you do it?”

“Oh, I don’t know. I’m feeling too good to move right now.”

“It’ll take them twenty minutes to get here. You have to be ready by then, okay?”

“Sure, whatever you say, Big Al.”

But even though he agreed, getting him to go back into his body did not seem probable. I couldn’t let this opportunity pass. There had to be a way. Maybe strong coffee. Was there a Heavenbucks? Like a genie, I tried to conjure a cup. Nothing.

I sat next to him and gave it some thought. After a few minutes I had an idea. There was no guarantee, but it was worth a shot. Grabbing his ears, I forced him to look at me.

“Ow! Hey, let go.”

"No, it's time for you to listen." I yanked his head back and forth a few times.

"Okay! Okay! I'll listen. Stop!"

I let go, but remained ready to resume my grip.

"Here's what you need to say: 'Bomb.' Repeat it."

Mac didn't respond so I pulled and twisted his ear. "Oww!"

"Repeat what I say, or I swear when you snap out of your coma you won't have any ears left. Let's try it again."

"Okay. Let go." He seemed to be sobering a bit.

"I'll let go when you finish. Now repeat after me. 'Bomb'."

"Bomb," he yelled. "You're really killing my buzz, Chance."

I twisted his ear. "Stop calling me Chance. Repeat 'concert'."

"Concert."

"'River View Park. Big Sound Systems. Truck. Acadia'."

Mac repeated it all but I was afraid he'd forget it once he got free of me. I made him say everything again.

"Bomb-concert-River View Park-Big Sound Systems-truck-Acadia."

We did it three more times. If he could keep it together for just a while longer, we'd succeed.

I sat and waited a few more minutes to make sure the cops arrived. Then something else came to me. Hipsher should not get away with killing me.

"Mac."

"What now? You gonna pull my ears again? What kind of guy pulls another guy's ears?"

"I promise I'm not gonna touch you. But I need to add

one more thing."

"Sure, why not? I'm not gonna remember any of it anyway."

That was all I could take. My anger, frustration, and desperation boiled together. I grabbed his shoulders and shook him, screaming in his face. "This is important. You weren't there. I was. It's the most horrible thing you could ever imagine. There was blood and-and body parts everywhere. The screams were so loud. The pain was everywhere. Mac, if you saw what I saw, you would be fighting to get back there and make someone listen."

I had been talking so fast and with such passion I didn't notice that Mac was quiet and staring at me. Something wet fell on my hand. Another drop followed. I touched my cheek; it was wet.

"Chance," his voice was calm. "Are you okay?"

"No, I'm not. I think I'll die if I don't save those people. I can't take it. The agony within me is so vast that I think it will kill my spirit for eternity. I've asked so much of you Mac, but please, we're so close. Just this one more time; I promise. You'll never see me again. Please!"

I was losing control of my emotions and my mind. This one moment was what my whole life and death had come down to.

"Okay, Chance. I'm feeling a lot better. I'll do this once more. I hope it works, but please, don't be here when I get done."

I stared at him in disbelief. Was saving thousands of lives so bad that I had to beg the only person who could assist me for help? And as a reward for my efforts, he banned me from further contact? Well, if that's how he wanted to be, so be it. All that mattered was that he got the message through.

I nodded.

"What's the other thing?'

I almost forgot. I swallowed hard and backhanded the tears away. "The cop who killed me is named Hipsher. If you get to it, fine. If not," I shrugged, "what's the difference? I'm dead anyway." With that, I blinked to the hospital room.

CHAPTER

Fifty-Six

Mac's father was the only one in the room at the time, parked in his usual spot. His hands were folded and his head down. He whispered a repeated prayer through the tears.

Pollen and O'Reilly hadn't appeared yet. I feared the timing would be all wrong. As I watched, Mac's body twitched then stiffened. The strain showed on his face. His heart rate began to rise fast. He was having trouble.

Mac's eyes opened for a second and locked with mine. "Oh, Chance," he said. Then they closed for what I feared would be the last time. The words chilled me. Fear grew sharper with each passing second.

Barney was on his feet and at his son's side in an instant. Shock and fear showed on his face as the monitor displayed the increasing heart rate.

I was afraid for Mac's life. I didn't want him to die. He needed to live. Not just for the people the bomb would take, but because he had been brave enough to try to save them. He risked his own life for them. Even though he might not like me, his actions spoke highly of him in my book.

I looked to the heavens. "God, please. I know I've asked before, but it's not for me. You know that. I've never been like that. Whether or not he can give the message please save him."

As the numbers flashed higher, an alarm went off. The room filled with nurses, including Beverly. They worked and communicated as a well-trained team. When Mac flat lined, they were ready with paddles in hand.

If Mac was gone, I had to catch him before his spirit left. I jumped to Mac's brain. It was dense with a strange fog. An eerie light glowed through the haze. I swam through the fog, trying to get closer to the light. The farther in I went, the more the angle of the light changed. It appeared to be coming from above.

I heard a whoosh and was drawn to the sight of Mac spinning in circles, arms outstretched and his head laid back, gazing in awe at the light. He was about to lift off for the hereafter. I couldn't allow that. As he lifted off I raced forward and yelled, "No, Mac!"

I launched at his legs and managed to wrap my arms around him. The pull from the light was strong. I only managed to slow his rise a bit. I was having trouble holding on. His body was becoming less dense.

"Mac, give the nurses a chance to save you. Don't give up yet!"

"Let go, Chance. I'm being called home."

Huh! I was never called home. I was just gone. I guess I knew where he was headed. *Forgive me, God, but you can't have him yet.* I pulled as hard as I could and for a moment began making progress, but someone up there must have turned up the power because we began to rise again.

"Mac, you're quitting too easy. Think of all the loved ones you're leaving behind. You can't desert them like this."

I wasn't sure if it was because of me or not, but we stopped rising. For a moment we hung there, suspended in nowhere land. Above me, Mac was looking downward past me. "Huh?" he said. He cocked his head then looked up. "Aw, man!" Then there was a bright flash and Mac was gone. I fell like I had weight, landing feet first.

I looked around, confused as to what had happened. The light was gone as was the fog. I looked up, wondering if they had some supersonic cosmic spirit puller. Mac was nowhere in sight. I had lost him. He was gone and it was my fault.

Not knowing what else to do and afraid of what I would find, I blinked back to the hospital room. The nurses were calmer now. The fight was over. Everyone stood around the bed looking at the body. The family was crying; one of the nurses was crying. I hung my head in shame for what I had done to Mac.

"I'm sorry, Mac. I didn't want this."

A voice filled my mind. "I know, Chance. When I was dead, I caught a glimpse. I understand so much better now."

The tears continued until, "Bomb. Concert."

I snapped my head up and stared in shocked amazement.

A collective gasp escaped the room. As one they stepped toward the bed.

"River View Park. Big Sound Systems." Mac's voice came through soft but clear.

O'Reilly and Pollen entered at that moment. Beverly rushed into O'Reilly's arms.

"Truck. Acadia."

"Jesus, what's going on here?" said Pollen.

"He's talking again," answered Caroline. Her cheeks were red, but the rest of her face was white, as if her body couldn't decide whether to be excited or to faint.

Beverly took O'Reilly's face in her hands and forced him to look at her. "Believe, Jim. He's trying to tell us something."

He pursed his lips and studied her face. Then he nodded and stepped past her, taking out his notebook.

In a voice that sounded free of pain, Mac repeated, "Bomb. Concert. River View Park. Big Sound System.

Truck. Acadia."

Just then Mac's eyes fluttered. His eyes struggled to open. He was fighting to wake up. My mouth gaped opened as I grew excited for him, but it was a mixed emotion. If he woke now, Hipsher would go free, but the momentary sadness I felt evaporated when I thought about Mac living and having a normal life. I cheered out loud for his return.

But as close as he was, Mac wasn't quite ready yet. He sighed and his body relaxed. Everyone in the room let out a deep breath as well.

Pollen turned to O'Reilly and shook his head. "This can't be real." He walked to the bed and bumped past Caroline, who was holding Mac's hand and whispering to him. A loud clap made everyone jump; everyone except the one person Pollen was hoping to see jump.

Barney barged around the bed and grabbed Pollen's arm as he was lightly smacking his son's face. He yanked Pollen back. "What the hell do you think you're doing? You leave my son alone."

Pollen appeared to be in shock. Whether it was over Mac's statement or Mr. MacIntosh's bold actions was unclear. O'Reilly stepped in and restored some calm to the room, pulling Pollen away from the bed.

"Mike, get a grip," O'Reilly whispered. "You may or may not believe," he looked at Bev, "but I do."

Bev beamed a teary-eyed smile.

"And at this point," O'Reilly said, "I don't think we can take a chance that there isn't some reality behind his words."

The room's inhabitants jumped again when Mac, his face twisted in pain, shouted out, "Hipsher killed Chance." His face contorted further. He let out a moan and was gone. No one in the room had their mouth open wider than me. For several seconds we all stared at Mac. Although nothing more happened, I let out a shout of joy. He had done it. Mac had laid the truth out there. Now it was up to these two fine detectives to run with it.

CHAPTER

Fifty-Seven

"Whoa!" Pollen said. "Did he just name his killer?"

"Oh, God!" O'Reilly answered. "I hope he didn't mean who I think he did." He began flipping back through his notes. He stopped at a page. His lips moved as he read to himself. When he was through he snapped his head up and stared at nothing.

"What?" asked Pollen.

O'Reilly held the notebook out for Pollen to read.

"Bomb-tomorrow-hurts-cop-swift-killed-Al-bomb-help-hurts.

Tomorrow-bomb-cop-killed-Chance-bomb-dead-bomb-many-help-police-

hurts-love-you-bomb."

Pollen looked up, his eyes displaying fear. He walked out of the room and O'Reilly followed. So did I.

"I was reading it as a cop was killed, maybe in the blast," said O'Reilly. "Or perhaps by this Chance. Maybe I was reading it wrong."

"This can't be. I mean, damn, we're talking about a cop here. You know what kinda shit storm this will cause if we're wrong? Just for suggesting it we could have the entire department down on us." He put his hand on his head and walked away. He stopped and came back. "We can't be wrong about this, Jim. We have to make sure."

"I agree. But the bomb comes first. If this is real, we have to stop it from going off."

"So the first thing we have to do is check out Swift's apartment. See if there's anything there that ties him to a bomb. We need something solid to bring to the boss. Then we head for this sound place on Acadia. Check to see if they exist. I'll check to see if there's a concert tonight in River View Park."

They both started pecking at the buttons on their phones. O'Reilly looked up first. "Big Sound Systems does exist and they are on Acadia."

Pollen met his eyes shaking his head. "There's a concert tonight. In the park. It's a big one. Bon Jovi. Opening act is at 7:30; Bon Jovi takes the stage around 9."

"Christ!" O'Reilly looked at his watch. We've got less than four hours. The place will be packed. Mike, we have to tell someone."

Pollen looked into the room at the miracle man lying in the bed. He truly didn't know what to believe. He wasn't sure he was willing to believe in ghosts or an afterlife, or that they can communicate with the living. The one thing he did believe in was his gut reaction, and right now, it was screaming at him to move.

He looked back at O'Reilly and nodded. "Let's go. I'll make the call on the way."

As they hastened down the hall, Beverly poked her head out and yelled after them. "Jim, I believe in you."

O'Reilly stopped and looked back. His expression told me that if the situation wasn't so dire, he would've rushed back and hugged her. Instead, he waved and ran to catch up to Pollen.

CHAPTER

Fifty-Eight

For the first time I had real hope that we might succeed. It was hard to hold back my excitement, but the threat wasn't over yet. I wanted to see how Mac was doing, but I had made him a promise. Instead, I went home. I wanted to share the news with someone and Les was the only soul I knew to talk to.

My space was empty except for the one picture on my invisible wall. I looked at that picture and realized that was the last time I had been close to anyone. They were the last people I called friends. When each of them died, I never wanted to feel that loss again. The pain was too great.

Sure, I met people and made friends, but I never got close to them. I never developed long lasting relationships. Of course, that could also be because I didn't stay in one place for very long.

But these guys were special. We shared life and danger together and developed a strong bond. We had each others' backs, and when it looked like we would all survive, we couldn't have been happier. We talked about what we would do when we got home. I still remember what some of the guys had in mind. None of us got our wishes, but we did have good times, shared with great friends. When they died, a large part of me died with them.

I turned away from the photo. I didn't have time for this. There was still work to be done, not by me, but I felt a need to look over the two detectives' shoulders like some sort of spirit supervisor.

I sat down on an invisible chair and floated. Starting at the beginning, I ran through everything I knew. I wanted to make sure I hadn't missed or overlooked something.

When I got to the part about Monica, I skipped over it. There was no sense in reliving what never was. The only way I could've been with her was if I'd never gone to the restaurant. Although that would've made my life heaven on earth, it would've destroyed thousands of other lives. I was willing to sacrifice that good life to save people I'd never met.

Still, I couldn't deny the draw to see her, if for only one more time. Out of curiosity, I jumped to the diner in the reality thread on the same day we would have met. I wanted to see what Monica's life would be like without me. I just wanted to know she would be happy. It was important to me.

I watched her say her goodbyes to the other staff and leave the diner. She turned in the same direction as before and walked up the street. Her head was down as she passed the alley where the terrorist bomber was. If he was still there, it was either because the detectives hadn't taken him down yet—or he'd escaped.

As Monica passed them, unaware of their presence, the three men moved toward her. With no one there to protect her she became a target. My chest tightened and my pulse quickened as the men closed in on her. I screamed and dove at them. I swung with everything I had but could not stop them from grabbing her up and dragging her back into the alley.

Monica screamed and they covered her mouth. She kicked, flailed, and bit, but in the end the attack was too strong and brutal. The men bore her into the alley where they gang raped her. Her cries for help had long died by the time they were through with her.

My heart burst into a million pieces. I loved this woman I had never met, but there was nothing I could do to save her. I sobbed uncontrollably. Les was right. Sometimes it was better to never know.

If that had been the end of her torment, it would've been enough to overcome and try to live a normal life. But the bastards took her with them. They shoved her half-naked into a van and drove her to a rundown apartment building. There they shot her up with a variety of drugs and then raped her again. This went on for the better part of three days, most of which Monica was too drugged out to know what was happening.

When the drugs began to run out they sold her for more drugs or money, ultimately pimping her out on the street as a prostitute. She no longer looked the same. Her future was gone in a more horrendous manner than mine ever could've been.

At least I had chosen my course of action, knowing full well the risks. Perhaps my fate had always been tied to that ambush in the desert years ago. My violent end was preordained since that day. Or maybe I had subconsciously been searching for that end as a form of dealing with survivor's guilt.

But Monica had not chosen this path. It had been forced on her. A beautiful life destroyed by sleaze that I should've killed in that alley days before. Her screams and anguish haunted me.

As if I didn't already have enough guilt on my conscience, now I had to shoulder the burden of Monica's living death. Because I died I wasn't there to walk her safely past the scum in that alley. The torture Monica would endure for the rest of her life was because of my failure.

I prayed God would banish me to anywhere else so I wouldn't have to face Monica when she died. I couldn't take it, knowing I had been responsible for her tortured existence.

Barely able to focus, I fled back to the safety of my cloud. I curled into the fetal position, my body trembling. I never wanted to move again. I was done.

CHAPTER

Fifty-Nine

"I'll tell you one thing," said Pollen. "Swift made good money doing whatever he was doing. This is not the apartment of a man with no money. His bank and checking accounts only show small balances and little activity. There's just enough money going in to cover his bills."

O'Reilly stood at the sliding balcony door and looked out over the city. They were on the twelfth floor of a very nice, if not quite luxury, apartment building. "And yet look around. The furnishings are minimal. There is nothing expensive here. He doesn't have any pictures or decorations anywhere. There's nothing here to tell us anything about the man. This is an apartment of someone ready to move at a moment's notice."

"The only picture is this one; I assume it's his platoon." Pollen held up the framed picture. He squinted at it. "That must be him there."

O'Reilly turned from the window. "There's nothing but clothes in the bedroom. The bathroom has only the basic necessities. The kitchen and refrigerator are stocked with food." He looked around the space and noticed a narrow table against the wall. He studied it for a moment before realizing what had drawn his attention.

"The computer's missing."

"What?"

"On the table. There's a cord for the internet, but no computer. It must be a laptop."

"Well, he sure didn't have it on him when we found his body."

The two men went through the apartment again, looking for the missing computer, but came up empty.

Pollen said, "So what does that mean? Either he had it with him and maybe that's why he was killed, or it's in the shop being repaired?"

"Or," O'Reilly said, "someone's been here and took it."

"We could ask for any surveillance video."

"Yeah, but let's tell them to hold it for us. I have a bad feeling about this. I think we need to get to that music equipment place now."

* * *

The two men left the apartment, closing the door. Five minutes later the sliding door opened and a man dressed in black entered carrying a laptop.

Dominic Marino, alias Roberts, picked up the photo and sighed. "So that's why you haven't been answering my calls. I'm sorry, buddy. I'll miss you."

He set the photo down. Opening the duffel bag he had slung across one shoulder, he slid the laptop inside and zipped it close. Dominic had just enough time to grab the computer and slip on to the balcony before the two cops entered. He couldn't allow the laptop to fall into their hands. Swifty kept too many files in the memory. Dominic had warned him that was a bad idea, but Chance wouldn't listen. He remembered Swifty's reply. "The only way someone's getting this computer is if I'm dead. And then it won't matter."

But it did matter to Dominic. The information inside this

laptop could lead the authorities to him. He'd spent too much time working under the radar to be brought down now. Too many people relied on him.

As Dominic exited the room he wondered what Swifty had been working on that got him killed. Hopefully it would be in the computer and would lead Dom to Chance's killer. He would avenge his friend. It was the least he could do. Then he would break open a bottle of Jameson's and drink to Chance's memory.

CHAPTER

Sixty

I wasn't sure how long I lay there oblivious to my surroundings. I'd say I was lost in thought, but I had banned thought from my mind. The only reason I came back into focus was because Les was standing over me calling my name. For some reason I couldn't ignore him. He was inside my head.

"Leave me alone, Les."

"Why, you hypocrite, you."

"Excuse me?"

"You heard me, you waste of space and time. All the while you've been here, all you've done is complain about not getting a chance to save some people. You yelled at me about not doing enough and almost killed poor Garrett. You harassed that boy because he wanted to quit. And here you lay, quitting on everyone else, when you actually have a chance to pull this thing off. At least Garrett had a reason for quitting. He was in severe, life-threatening pain. You're just a quitter."

"Les, did you know what they were gonna do to her?"

Les got quiet. "I tried to warn you that you might not like what you see. For what it's worth, I'm truly sorry. But I don't mean to be cruel here. There may not be anything you can do to save her, but you still have a chance to rescue all those people from being blown up."

He squatted next tome. "Now, are you going to see this thing through or are you going to pout like a little baby?"

I almost decided to lay there and do the pout thing, but then something Les said sprouted an idea in my head. *'There may not be anything you can do to save her...'* Was that Les' way of telling me there was still a chance, or was he just trying to motivate me? I thought about it for a moment and decided he was giving me a hint. Real or not, I wanted—no, needed—to believe in that possibility.

Then it came to me, hitting my feeble mind like a freight train. What I had seen was Monica's future. It hadn't happened yet. Her ordeal was still a few hours away. I still had a chance to save her if Pollen and O'Reilly could stop the bomb and capture that terrorist. The excitement was so thick I could taste it.

With fresh hope, I stood up and faced him. "I know what you did for Bev and O'Reilly, you little matchmaker, you."

With a completely straight face, Les said, "I have no idea what you are talking about."

"Right. Someday you need to teach me that trick. Okay transition counselor, I need to get to work. Close the door on your way out."

CHAPTER

Sixty-One

Now it was up to two detectives I had never met to believe in something they had never thought real before to stop the bombers from killing thousands and destroying Monica's life.

I knew what had to be done. I could still save Monica. I set a new cosmic speed record in getting to Mac's soul light, but when I arrived something had changed. The light no longer extended away from the Earth. It was a short solid circle. Worse than that, it was impenetrable. No matter how hard I tried I could not enter Mac's brain. I checked every inch, tried every possible angle, but I could not get in.

I kicked and pounded and screamed out Mac's name. Nothing worked. Had Mac shut me out? I knew he was upset with me, but after his near death event I thought maybe he had relented. Maybe he was mad because I didn't check on him after his last reentry, but I thought that's what he wanted. Besides, I promised I wouldn't bother him again even though here I was again, bothering him.

But this was important. It was every bit as important as the bomb was. Mac had to let me in. I was desperate. I begged Mac. I begged Les. I begged God and anyone else I could think of. No one answered and I was not allowed to enter.

Maybe Mac had died. The strain could have been too much for him. Great! Add that guilt to the rest.

Finally, I beamed into the hospital room. The family was

still there and they were taking turns pacing the small space. Beverly was discussing Mac's pain meds with the doctor. Mac was being weaned off the large dosage. That told me that Mac was still alive, but he was shutting me out. I had lost my only ally. I couldn't be mad. Mac had been through a lot for me. I was pained because I knew what that meant, but there was nothing I could do. All hope faded away. I had lost the fight to save Monica.

"Okay, Mac. I wish you a full recovery and a long and happy life. Look me up some day," I said.

One slim chance remained to save Monica, but it relied on two detectives who I could no longer communicate with. I had to find them. Time was running out.

I pictured the warehouse and jumped there. The truck was gone. Out front it was business as usual. The man working the counter was either a very good actor or wasn't involved in the plot. His interaction with the customer was too casual. Right now he wasn't important. I needed to know the exact placement of the bomb.

I waited to see if the detectives showed up. Impatience got the best of me though, and a few minutes later I moved on to the bomb site. It wasn't like I could lead the detectives to any clues anyways, but for my own quickly fading sanity, I needed to know they stopped the men who would destroy Monica. Even an arrest may be enough to alter Monica's destiny.

If I were alive and found him, I'd rip his head off. But then I'd never felt bound by too many laws, otherwise I'd never been able to help the people I did. There was right, then there was wrong. I didn't let laws stand in the way of deciding how to deal with wrong.

My stomach did flip-flops. Nausea swept over me,

although I'm sure it was only a memory of that feeling. Desperation grew with each tick of time that passed.

Finding the stage, I floated toward it. I saw no sign of the truck. Where had it gone? Was it still on the road or had it been there, deadly shipment dropped off, and gone already?

I looked around for any of the equipment I saw at the warehouse. So much was piled up behind the stage that it was difficult to tell. At least fifty people moved around the stage working on various parts of the construction. None of them was the man I sought.

I clapped hands to face and tried to think. The only way to know for sure where the truck went was to jump back in time to the warehouse and follow it. It would be more wasted time, but there really wasn't an alternative.

Just then, a truck entered through a temporary gate at the far end of the site. BSS was in large letters on the door. I felt relief and panic all at once. I'd found the man who would kill so many and destroy my love, but how was I going to stop him? Where were those damn cops?

The truck moved behind the stage and parked. The sight of the driver sent wild flames of rage through me. I wanted to kill him. I wanted him dead right now, not just for my own deserved revenge. I wanted it for Monica and for the thousands of lives lost and the families their loss would destroy.

Without thought, I launched at him as if I were a missile. I passed through him, trying to will myself solid. There had to be a way. Les might know how, just like he somehow brought Bev and O'Reilly together, but I doubted he would tell me if he did.

My only reward for the attack was a brief pause in the killer's step. He knit his brows and looked around, then touched the back of his neck and began walking again.

Excited by what I perceived as a possibility, I tried again. This time I passed through his back and stopped in front of his face. I unloaded everything I had at his body without effect. I willed my fists to take solid form with every ounce of strength I had, fueled by hatred so strong I could smell it in the air.

Just one fist; just one punch. That was all I asked and all I needed. It was a frenzied, all-out desperate attack threatening to drive me further towards the madness encompassing me.

I had no effect on him. My rage and frustration grew. I was beyond control or rational thought. I screamed, clawed, and bit in a savage assault but in the end, the rear gate still lifted and the bomber began moving equipment out of the truck.

I dropped to my knees and pounded my fists on the ground. *God, how can you let this happen?* I watched helplessly as piece after piece was unloaded. Men came and carried the monitors, lights, and speakers up to the stage. Like a human conveyor belt, the equipment passed from man to man and placed into position.

Slowly the frame of the stage took shape. Massive columns of speakers were erected. Some were placed on the ends of the stage while others were raised in the air. Men climbed the scaffolding to adjust the multicolored spotlights. Others began hoisting the backdrop into place.

I watched from above, helpless to prevent the show from going on. Time passed with still no sign of the police.

When the truck was nearly empty, the bomber pulled the overhead door down and rode the lift to the ground.

“Is that it?” one of the workers said.

“Yeah,” replied my hated foe. “The rest goes out front.”

With a wave he climbed back into the truck and drove to the sound control tent. The raised platform had a canopy covering the top and sat about fifty yards off center stage. One man was on the platform setting up tables.

The mass murderer carried massive sound boards, cables, and other equipment up the wooden steps. The sound engineer had him place the boards where he wanted then began connecting cords. The two men discussed the components, but whatever they were saying was beyond my technological knowledge or interest.

Toothless said, “Isn't this a little late to be setting up? When are they going to do the sound check?”

“The bands plane got delayed. They're skipping the sound check. I'm going to adjust levels while opening act is playing. Bon Jovi has their own sound guy who will set them up between acts. It'll be tight, but what can you do.”

“Well, good luck with that,” toothless said, then went down to the truck.

The last item unloaded was the rolling storage crate. A chill ran through me as I watched. The bomber opened the crate and looked in. He stared glassy eyed for a moment then shook himself from the spell. He shut the lid and locked the box, then rolled the crate down the ramp, but instead of going up on the sound stage, Toothless pushed it under the wooden structure.

“I’m just going to leave this here for later, okay?” he said.

“Sure. No problem,” the technician replied without looking up from his work.

Toothless smiled; the missing tooth evident. He drove away with no one there to stop him. I scanned the area, searching for the detective as my hope evaporated. Hope had been nothing but a very unsatisfying roller coaster ride. I had failed—again.

CHAPTER

Sixty-Two

My only chance now was to try Mac one more time. In a flash, I was outside the faint cone of light that was Mac's life force. The cone was a little bigger than last time. The sight gave me new hope. The roller coaster ride continued. I might have a better chance of entering now.

I struggled but couldn't break through whatever barrier had been erected against me. I stepped back and studied the light. There had to be a way in. I moved to the very top of the cone and tried to use it as a reverse megaphone.

"Mac, can you hear me? I found the bomb. Please Mac, one last time."

It might have been my imagination, but I thought the cone grew wider. Just a bit, so I increased my efforts. "Mac, help me. Make contact one more time to tell them where it is."

Words floated upward, but I couldn't make them out. If it was Mac, his voice was very weak. I feared he had reached the end of his life. I was too late to save everyone and had most likely contributed to Mac's death as well.

I strained to hear what Mac was saying.

"Chance." He said my name.

"Yes, Mac, it's me. Please let me in."

"I'm sorry Chance. I tried."

I sobbed for his loss. "I know, Mac. I know you did. I'm sorry too."

"Chance." He called again.

Suddenly, I was falling through the light. At the very bottom, Mac was reaching toward me. He had an agonized look on his face. His body was fading away. He was dying. I reached him and touched his hand for a just a second. His eyes widened. Fear glazed his eyes.

"I'm here for you, brother."

His face relaxed. His eyes met mine "It's all right, Chance." Then a warm smile crossed his face, taking the pained look away. Bathed in an angelic glow he looked transcendent.

"Goodbye, Chance." And he was gone.

The light was gone. I was standing alone in the dark. "I'm so sorry, Mac."

I was about to head home, not wanting to witness the carnage I had seen before. As an afterthought, I decided to beam into Mac's hospital room once more, like a funeral attendee viewing the body of a dear friend. I braced myself for the grief stricken room and blinked into my usual corner. The family was gathered around the bed crying. Mac's mother was holding one hand. The father had his hands on the blankets covering Mac's legs. Caroline's head was on Mac's chest.

It was as I expected—a family in mourning for the loss of a loved one. As expected, except for one thing.

"Caroline, I can't breathe."

A sobbed laugh escaped Caroline as she lifted her head. "I'm sorry. I'm just so happy. I can't help it." With that, she plopped her head back down on Mac's chest.

My soul soared, if a soul could have a soul. Mac was alive. I shouted for joy and cried unabashedly. He made it back. I did an aerial flip. It was an emotional time for everyone. I was happy for him, yet sad as well. So much had depended on Mac. It wasn't fair to him to have had such a huge burden placed upon his struggling shoulders. I had put him through a lot. He had not only been fighting for his own life, but for thousands of others he had never met. It was a shame that his painful sacrifices would be all for naught. But at least one person would survive.

As Caroline moved so Mac's mother could slide in for a hug, Mac looked over her shoulder, up at my corner, as if he were looking for me. I smiled. It had to be my imagination. I was sure our connection was broken. In fact, Mac would probably have no recollection of what he had been through in his near death struggle. To him it would be nothing more than a bad dream. Hopefully, he would not be able to recall any of it. Why should he have to live with that kind of traumatic memory?

"Good luck, Mac." I was about to leave when Mac winked toward me. I froze. A smile came to his face. "Don't worry," he said. "Everything is gonna be all right."

For a brief instant my heart beat faster. I thought he was talking to me, but then, his mother placed a hand on each side of Mac's face and said, "I know, honey. I know."

CHAPTER

Sixty-Three

After leaving Mac I floated in nowhere zone for a while. I had to get control of my emotional overload. My mental state of late was so strange. After the ambush, I had become an emotionless rock. Oh, I cared and tried hard to make sure innocent people didn't suffer their own emotional setbacks. But my only emotion seemed to be a controlled, but constant, anger. The lack of ability to control the outcome of a given situation had rendered me a blubbering mass of raw emotion. Not only couldn't I control my surroundings but I couldn't control myself, either.

After seeing things through to this point, I couldn't turn my back now. I floated back toward the concert grounds. Only about two hours remained before the concert would begin. Four hours before the bomb would explode. It was going to take a miracle to stop this act of terrorism now. I could ask for one but I didn't think I was high enough on the totem pole to have my request granted or even listened to.

Of course, I was in the realm of the miracle, so it was worth a try. Without knowing where to start I decided to check in with my transition guide—if he was still taking my calls.

Back on my cloud, I shouted out. "Hey Les, if you got a minute I'd appreciate some advice."

"Wow!" The voice shocked me. "That was different."

I grabbed my chest as if I actually still had a beating heart. "Damn, man! Why do you have to sneak up on me like that all the time?"

"If you weren't on edge all the time you wouldn't get spooked by my dropping in."

"Yeah, right. Spooked by a spook. Good one."

"To what do I owe the honor of this almost polite request?"

I looked at him and felt some of the tension dissipate. "I'm sorry if I've been rude. I got so involved in thinking I could make a difference that I got a little annoying."

"A little?"

I barked a laugh. "Yeah, thanks. Okay, I guess I was a little crazed."

He flashed his teeth. "Yes, but as you said before, with good intent. I take it things haven't worked out for you. I'm sorry. Is that why the call?"

"You mean you haven't been monitoring my progress?"

"Contrary to your belief that I am here for you solely, I do have other charges I need to check in with. Have you run into a problem?"

"Yeah, things didn't turn out the way I had hoped. Only a miracle or divine intervention can save those people now."

Les nodded his head as if agreeing. "So this call isn't social. You want to ask me how to have a miracle granted, right?"

"You're a really smart man, Les. You know that?"

"Of course I know that. I'm just surprised it took you this long to understand that." He smiled again.

"So what do you think my chances are?"

"I'm sorry to say, but nil. I mean, I don't have a say in these things, but miracles are very rare. Miracles are usually huge events that send a message of hope to the masses. Divine intervention is more common and most of the time few people are aware that something amazing has occurred. Unfortunately, neither of us has a say in whether an intervention is approved, let alone considered."

"But if it were considered, how would I do it? Who do I talk to?"

"It's passed upward through channels. Channels that you, as a temporary resident here, have no access to."

"What about you? Don't you have any access to these channels?"

"More so than you do, but even still, I'm only a temp here as well."

"Speaking of which, how long have you been here?"

Les looked down. A strange and troubled look came to his face. "By earth standards, twenty-seven years."

"What? Why so long?"

He pondered for a moment before answering. "It just has."

"I don't understand. Surely you've spent enough time here for the Powers That Be to determine if you're worthy of entrance into heaven or the next level or whatever. What's the hold up?"

"Ah, it's complicated."

I studied his face. Some inner turmoil roiled behind those intelligent eyes.

"You do want to move on, don't you?"

"Of course I do." But he cleared his throat as if the words were stuck there.

"I have to be ready first. They'll let me know when I am."

Something Les said a while back came to mind. "You said I was the last one. If you succeed with me, then you're done here. Is that right?"

He gave a noncommittal shrug.

"What if I screw up? Will you have to do another lost soul?"

"I suppose. I'm sure they'll inform me should that be the case."

"Man; this is so unfair. Everyone's future depends on me." Talk about heavy responsibilities. "But what if I make it? You'll be reunited with your wife. Isn't that what you want?"

Les didn't speak. That was it. He was afraid to see her again. In his mind he would never be able to atone for not being there for her when she needed him. He still blamed himself for her death.

I put my arm on his shoulder to be comforting. To my surprise, it rested there as if on something solid. Could I touch him or I had I merely adjusted to the situation? "It's time for you to move on. I don't want to be the cause of you having to stay. It's not fair that my failure should be yours."

He didn't say anything for a moment and I dropped my arm.

"Anyway," he said, "I'll pass along your request but seriously, don't get your hopes up. I'm sorry to say that after all the effort you've gone to, but the truth is, sometimes bad things happen for reasons we may never understand. Even here, understanding is not complete."

"I understand that."

"I promise I'll do what I can."

"That's all I can ask. I do appreciate everything you've done for me." I stuck out my hand. He looked at it, and then accepting the gesture for what it was, put his in mine. We shook. Then he smiled and was gone.

CHAPTER

Sixty-Four

"Oh my God, Swifty, what the hell did you get yourself involved in?" Dominic Marino sat staring at the screen of his partner's laptop. "Is this real?" he said aloud. He was in his small, but nice two bedroom home in the suburbs. As the schematics of a bomb appeared, Dominic had to think about how well he knew Chance Swift.

"Tell me this isn't yours, my friend. You would never build a bomb, would you?" He pushed another key and more information scrolled before him. "Oh geez! Are these arming codes? Why do you have this on your computer?"

Marino stood and rubbed his face, unsure of what to do or think. If the bomb was real, he had to tell someone, didn't he? He needed a beer. Dominic walked to the kitchen, opened the refrigerator, and grabbed a cold bottle. He stopped for a moment, then put it back. This called for something a little stronger. He reached up, opened a cupboard and withdrew a bottle of Kentucky bourbon. He half-filled a water glass and gulped the liquid down. He started back to the den, stopped and refilled the glass, then continued. Taking another large drink, he sat down then popped right back up. He couldn't sit; he had to think, and thinking was done best on your feet.

No way would his friend be involved in this. Dominic knew Chance Swift too well. However, it could very well be what got him killed. And if someone was willing to kill for this, then the bomb had to exist. Now the question was, what should he do with the information?

No way could he just hand the drive over to the police. They would want to know too much about him and how he came into possession of the information. If he got arrested for some reason, he would be of little value to the people who needed him most- those who needed the police's help, but for one reason or another couldn't afford to involve or get involved with them.

So what to do, or better yet, what would Swifty do?

* * *

Like the TV show, I Jeanied myself to the concert site. Nothing appeared to have changed, other than the stage was more built up and the massive speakers were now in place. No sign of the bomber or a police presence. Dismayed, my anger flared again. But in spite of the reality, I still retained a spark of hope. Maybe God would grant a last-minute stay in the form of an intervention. I tried not to think about it.

As I tried to decide what to do, I noticed people were already gathering at the entrance. A little more than an hour before show time and there were nearly a thousand fans in line outside the temporary chain link fencing erected around the grounds.

I looked toward the sky, praying for a last minute thunderstorm that might cancel the concert, but no such luck was to be mine. The show was gonna happen. With no help in sight, I went to BS Systems.

Nothing was going on there either. In fact, the store was closed. The guy running the counter out front was talking in a very animated way to someone on the phone.

"No, I'm telling you the police were just here."

"....What do you mean, 'what did I tell them?' What is there to tell? What have you gotten into?"

"....Yeah, they asked about the truck and the concert so I told them you and the truck were at the concert grounds now. What did you do, get a speeding ticket or run a red light?"

"....Look, I don't want any problems with the police. If you did something head out of town, just bring the truck back now.... Huh? No, they left. I think they were heading to the concert site."

"Hello! Hello, Ali? Shit!" He slammed the phone down.

So the cops had arrived and found nothing. That meant a chance still existed they might find the bomb. I rushed back to the park. Standing on the stage, I searched the area. The crowd outside the fenced area was growing by the minute.

As I watched, the delivery truck entered and drove toward the sound control platform. Three men got out and walked at a hurried pace toward the elevated structure. I sped toward them, recognizing the trio; Toothless and my other two attackers.

The tall man, I guessed was Ali, said, "The police are on their way. I'm not sure what they know, but they are looking for the truck. I'm going to drive it away and hide it somewhere. You two stay here and look as though you're working. Don't do anything to draw attention to the crate. But if anyone goes near it, stall them as long as you can." He scanned the perimeter. A smile came to his face when he saw the size of the crowd gathering. He said almost to himself, "This is going to be bigger than I had imagined."

He gave a furtive look in all directions then glanced up at the sound tech. Squatting, he opened the crate, reached in and seconds later closed and locked the lid. I didn't have to look to know he had just armed the bomb. He stood, scanned the crowd again, smiling once more.

The smile faded and he turned to his two accomplices. “Whatever happens you have to be away from here by nine. You understand?”

Both men nodded and glanced under the platform nervously. The shorter one said, “What if the authorities come?”

“Try to stall them and answer their questions. Stay relaxed. If they persist, run into the crowd and lose them. With this many people it should be easy. Make your way to the exit and escape. You know where to go.”

The two men nodded but were clearly unhappy.

“You are both armed. If you have to, you kill the police to stop them from opening that box. Shoot them and run. You will be the distraction that draws them away. I must go now, my friends. We will meet later. Good luck.” He climbed into the cab and started for the gate.

Maybe that was how he had escaped the police and was waiting for Monica.

CHAPTER

Sixty-Five

I watched, anxious for any sign of the police. By now I should've heard sirens coming from every direction in the city. I was tempted to fly the route between the park and the music store to see if there were any donut shops along the way.

A few minutes later they arrived. I was excited even though they were ten minutes late. The truck was long gone.

The unmarked car stopped at the gate. Pollen talked for a while to the guard there before entering the grounds. He drove to the stage and the two detectives exited the car. O'Reilly got on the phone while Pollen began flashing his badge at everyone he saw. I decided to float over and listen in.

Pollen had found someone who claimed to be in charge. Wesley Dalton was a large man wearing a tie and shirt with rolled up sleeves. He stood listening, hands on hips with obvious impatience. As I drew closer, the man swept an arm toward the stage.

"Yeah, just about every piece of equipment up there belongs to them. Is there gonna be a problem? I've got a show to put on in less than two hours. The gates open in about an hour. Look at all those people out there. If I've got to replace this stuff I need to know now."

Pollen pushed his jacket back and placed his hands on his hips. "I'm not sure there is a problem, but I need to check it out. Until then no one comes through those gates."

"What's the problem? Did they steal the speakers or something?"

Pollen stepped forward and lowered his voice. "Yeah, well look, I don't want to start a panic, but there's an outside chance there may be a bomb here somewhere. I've got a coupla teams on their way with trained bomb-sniffing dogs. We should know real soon if there's a problem."

"A bomb!" he shouted.

"Hey, keep your voice down. I want you to go up there and tell all the workers to take a break. Get them all back there behind those trailers." He pointed toward the three mobile homes brought in to house the bands and their staffs behind the stage.

Dalton wrung his hands, growing more nervous by the moment.

"Hey, Mr. Dalton, do you hear me? Get going, but don't start a panic."

The man did all he could not to run for the stairs. A few minutes later the entire stage reverberated with the sound of running. Men and women poured down the stairs. Some jumped from the platform. So much for preventing a panic.

O'Reilly came over. "I've got a locate-and-detain out on the truck. A patrol car is gonna stay at the store in case it shows up there. I've got a coupla cars coming to reinforce the security guys at the gate."

Pollen scratched his head. "Man, I hate to say it, but I hope we find something or we're gonna look awful foolish."

"The Chief wasn't real happy when all I could give him was a high probability tip from a reliable source," O'Reilly said. "He said if it wasn't me he'd say bring more proof. But if it doesn't pan out I'll be in big trouble. Something better be here, even if it's just an M-80."

"I just hope it doesn't go off while we're standing here waiting." he spun in a circle. "what if this nut job is watching and can remote detonate the device?"

"Aw, man, you had to bring that up, didn't you?"

They climbed the stairs and walked across the stage. Pollen walked to one of the speaker columns and examined it. He couldn't tell without opening the speaker up if anything was hidden inside.

I watched with nervous expectation. How long would it take for them to reach the control platform? When would those dogs arrive? The crowd was getting anxious as show time drew close. A constant, annoying buzz played out across the park. Just then music blared through the speakers. The crowd roared. Then it ceased. The tech scratched his head and searched for something.

The crowd booed.

Ten minutes later, when no one moved toward the sound stage, I booed too.

CHAPTER

Sixty-Six

By the time the dogs arrived, the crowd outside the gate had swelled to double-digit thousands. Instead of the excitement of seeing a great concert, they were now abuzz with the sight of seeing dogs sniffing around the stage.

An hour had passed by the time the dogs finished their job. Neither of the two trained canines found a hint of explosives.

I was desperate now. There had to be something I could do to direct their attention toward the sound booth. I was trying to come up with a solution when a policeman escorted Mr. Dalton to the stage.

"So what's the verdict?" He didn't seem to be as edgy now.

Pollen looked embarrassed. "We haven't found anything yet." He looked around as if searching for somewhere else to check.

"So if you haven't found anything, can I finish setting up and open the gates? I'm about a half hour late as it is."

To reinforce his statement, the crowd began to chant, "Let us in! Let us in!"

"You're gonna cause a riot. I'm not gonna be responsible if someone gets trampled to death."

I didn't wait for the answer. Instead I rocketed toward the smaller canvas-covered stage. There had to be something I could do. I had the ghost of an idea. The sound tech was busy inserting a huge array of wires into the motherboard.

Two other men were doing the same with the lighting and special effects boards.

I leaned over the rail and saw my two assailants just hanging around below, shooting nervous glances toward the stage.

A thunderous roar erupted from the crowd. I turned to see the gates had been opened. That meant they were giving up the search. I looked back at the lines of people streaming in. The cops were quitting and going home. I couldn't let that happen.

I was glad no one informed the sound guy about a possible bomb threat. He was still up there working. Walking up behind the sound tech, I watched his progress. I waited until he had a cord ready to insert into the board and then I passed into him. I stayed right inside his body. The hairs on the back of his neck sprung to attention and goosebumps erupted all along his body. He jumped, and as I hoped touched the wire to the side of the channel, sending a long, piercing squelch over the grounds.

* * *

The two detectives walked to the front of the stage and looked out as the crowd and began claiming their territory to watch the show from. Pollen shook his head. "I can't believe it. We're gonna look like chumps."

O'Reilly tilted his head and frowned as if to say, it is what it is. "I'm not sure what bothers me more; the fact that we wasted our time or that there was no bomb. The worst part is gonna be facing …" A high pitched noise made him wince and he covered his ears.

Pollen pointed at the distant stage. "What is that?"

"It's where they control the sound and lights."

"There's an awful lot of equipment there."

O'Reilly looked at Pollen, who shrugged. "Well, we don't have anything better to do."

* * *

Everyone flinched and covered their ears. The crowd hooted at the tech as they filed inside the grounds. I looked at the stage expectantly and waited. My heart pounded and my breathing went rapid. If I was alive I would've been on the brink of a heart attack.

I saw Pollen point in my direction. I couldn't help it; I waved my arms wildly over my head like Gilligan trying to catch the attention of a passing plane. Minutes passed slowly like an eternity, which didn't seem like a long time to me anymore. Then the entire troop descended the stairs of the main stage. O'Reilly whistled and waved to the dog handlers. A brief discussion ensued, then the dogs were unloaded again. The entire procession walked toward the sound stage. I jumped up and down, hooting like a kid at Christmas.

Glancing over the rail, the two bombers noticed the advance of the police and began talking at the same time. One pulled out a gun, but the other cautioned him and he replaced the weapon behind his back. I noticed that both men had begun to perspire. They disappeared under the stage and came out on the other side out of view of the police. Trying to remain casual, they walked away from the stage to mingle with the growing mob.

The dog handlers led their four-legged partners up the stairs. Five minutes later, having detected nothing, they came back down.

I screamed at them, “Under the stage! Look under the stage!” but to no avail. They were going to leave. I couldn't believe I'd gotten them so close only to fail in the end.

The canine team leader said, “Nothing. You got anywhere else you want me to check before we head out?”

Pollen and O'Reilly looked at each other, but neither spoke.

“Okay, then,” the leader said, “We're out of here.” they turned and started away from the platform.

In a last desperate effort, I dropped to the crate and began whistling at the dogs. I waved my arms across the top of the bomb in hopes of wafting the scent in their direction.

Just when I thought all hope had faded, one of the dogs turned, sniffed the air and caught a scent. She began barking. Seconds later the other dog joined in, straining against its leash. The handlers gave the dogs their head and let them lead. Pollen and O’Rielly glanced at each other and everyone moved back toward the sound stage.

At the structure the dogs went wild and led their handlers straight toward the crate. Pollen lifted his badge and called to the sound control man. “Is this your equipment?”

The tech leaned over the railing and looked down. “No, I rent it from a company. Why? Is there a problem?”

Pollen glanced at one of the handlers. The man nodded to Pollen.

“Yeah, there’s a big problem. I need you to come down here right now.” The man glanced at the soundboard and frowned. He set down the cord he was plugging in and descended the wooden stairs.

“Who do you get the equipment from?”

“Ah, Big Sound Systems. They deliver the stuff and I set it up. When the show is over they come back and pick it all up."

Pollen studied the man. "When was the last time you saw anyone from Big Sound?"

"Well, there were two of them hanging out down here a while ago. That's kind of unusual though. No one ever stays with the gear. They haul it out of the truck and go. Maybe they just wanted to see the concert for free."

"How long ago did you last see them?"

"Just a few minutes ago." The man gazed around. He caught sight of something and pointed. "I think that's them over there heading toward the gate."

Pollen grew excited. He couldn't allow them to get away. "Okay sir, I need you to go with these officers. Point out the two men for them." Turning to one of the officers he said, "Take him and stop those men."

The policeman nodded and began giving orders. With the sound tech trailing behind, four cops took off at a sprint.

Pollen turned his attention to the bomb sniffing dogs.

"We've got a bomb!" one dog cop announced.

I floated above them, cheered, and did aerials.

"Shit!" Pollen exclaimed.

Gunshots erupted. The group ducked. The fleeing men turned on the cops and opened fire. The crowd's scream erupted, their combined voices rising as one. They tried to flee all at once, but the humanity was too dense for anyone to move. Many of them dove for the ground, while several took bullets.

The pursuing officers drew their weapons. One twisted sideways and fell, taking a bullet in the shoulder. The police, unable to return fire for fear of hitting the crowd, were caught in the open. The two terrorists were without the same restraints as the police and fired in a steady assault, unconcerned about who they shot. Magazines empty, they reloaded and merged with the panicked masses pushing toward the gate.

Gunshots, screams, and shouts by the police trying to clear the crowd caused a chaos that filled the grounds as loud as any concert could have.

The two cops positioned outside the gate lined up shots from behind their squad car. They couldn't shoot but there was no way the two terrorists could get past them. The two men fired several rounds at the car but were forced to turn away. They ran toward the far edge of the grounds toward a line of vendors' trucks and carts, taking refuge behind a vendor selling fresh squeezed lemonade.

Now the shooters were more isolated. Although they had cover, the police no longer had to worry about a mass of innocent bystanders catching errant bullets. The gunfight intensified as the police moved to pen the two men in. Other cops herded the fans already inside the grounds in the opposite direction. A mass evacuation had begun under fire. It gave me a quick flashback to the war.

The two gunmen made a sudden dash from cart to cart while taking only light fire. Many of the booths were still occupied by vendors and their staff. It was at one of those food booths selling elephant ears, the two men stopped and took hostages. With the gunfight now at a stalemate, I turned my attention back to the bomb.

CHAPTER

Sixty-Seven

The bomb squad commander arrived and said, “Okay, my scene. I need all of you to back away and evacuate the entire area. That includes the entire park. Now, people! Move!”

Pollen and O’Reilly backed away. I followed. Pollen saw the smile on O’Reilly’s face. “What the hell are you so happy about?”

“Bev was right. Do you know what that means?” he locked eyes with Pollen.

“That you're gonna get laid again?”

O'Reilly smirked. “No! I mean, well yeah, but even more important. There is another side. There is life after death. The implications are life altering.”

“All I know is that some coma guy made some statements that led us to a bomb. In my mind there’s only one way he could’ve known. He was involved.”

“Oh come on, Mike. No way he could be involved. We checked him out. We found no trace on him or in his apartment. The guy’s been in a coma for almost a week. He didn’t transport or place that bomb there.”

“That just means he had accomplices.” He nodded toward the standoff in the distance. “We’ll know soon enough when we get those two in an interrogation room.”

“If we can get them into an interrogation room. And for the record, I think you’re wrong.”

Before Pollen could respond, the bomb squad

commander called out. “Hey!” He motioned to the two detectives and they jogged over. At the crate the commander said, “We’ve got a problem.” He pointed inside. The interior was filled with a large device. Red blinking numbers counted down. Less than two hours remained before detonation. “What information do you have on this bomb?”

O'Reilly said, “Not much. We had a tip, but little information to go on. We weren’t sure the bomb existed, but felt we had to check it out.”

“It’s on a timer but looks as though it took a code number to arm it. If that’s the case, it might take one to disarm it. If you can find that from whoever your source was, it will make this a whole lot easier. To be honest I’m not sure we can disarm it before it goes boom. As you can see, it’s a big ass bomb. This would've killed a lot of people.”

“It’s on wheels; can’t we just roll it out of here to some remote area?” Pollen said

“That’d be nice, but until I look this thing over to determine if it's got a motion trigger on it, I’m not moving it. It could also be rigged for remote detonation.” He shook his head. “I’ve got a bad feeling about this one. The best thing you can do is get everyone as far from here as possible. And that includes you two. Now if you’ll excuse me, I’ve got a lot of work to do and little time to do it.”

Pollen said, “We’ll do some digging.”

“Okay. The sooner, the better.”

A steady stream of police cars and fire trucks were arriving on scene as the detectives took off on a run for their car. No way was I missing this. In the car, O’Reilly called Bev and learned that Mac had recovered consciousness. He was weak but alert.

"Good," said Pollen. "Maybe now we can get some answers."

"I still think he's clean. We better start thinking of alternatives."

O'Reilly's phone rang. He answered and listened. "Okay, search the area and see if there is any video anywhere. I need a picture of this guy. Thanks." He hung up. "They found the truck in a Meijer parking lot. The driver was gone."

"I'd be willing to bet the two back there aren't the ones who built that bomb," Pollen said.

"My thoughts, too. The mastermind is still out there."

"What do you think about Hipsher being a part of all this?"

"Man, I hate thinking about it. I never really liked the guy, but how does a cop throw everything away and get involved in something like this? I need to make a call and have him brought in for questioning." He sighed. "I better inform the Captain. Man, is he ever gonna go nuts."

Pollen smiled. "Yeah, but not at us now."

Pollen spent the remainder of the drive on the phone explaining the situation to his boss and making arrangements. Even at high speed, the ride still took twenty minutes to reach the hospital. Twenty minutes closer to an explosion, but if the bomb went off now, at least there would be fewer victims. I had succeeded, almost. The image of Monica in that apartment with those men killed the elation I had been feeling over finding the bomb. There had to be something I could do. She would be leaving the diner soon.

A policeman stood guard outside the hospital room door. Mac's bed was angled upward a bit. Barney was gone, but Sandra and Caroline talked, clutched, and sobbed over an exhausted and frail looking Mac.

When O'Reilly and Pollen entered the room Mac smiled weakly. "I've been expecting you."

"Why, 'cause you knew we'd figure out you were involved?" Pollen said.

O'Reilly had the officer escort the women out of the room, but they didn't go without a fight or threat of arrest if they didn't leave.

Mac's smile faded. "Did you find a bomb?"

"You know we did. Now why don't you come clean about your part in this plot?"

Mac frowned. "You know that's not true. You just can't bring yourself to believe where I got the information. And it's the need for information that's brought you back, isn't it?"

Just then Beverly walked in. "Jim, what are you doing? He just woke from a coma. He's too weak to be interrogated." She hurried past the two detectives and began checking vitals. The doctor will have a cow if he finds you in here. You have to go."

Pollen put his hands on his hips, ready to go on the offensive. "Hey, listen ..."

O'Reilly held up a hand to stop him. "Bev, we found the bomb."

Her mouth gaped and she looked at Garrett then back to O'Reilly. "Oh, my God!" She stood in awe as the depth of the ramifications of that statement became clear. She snapped out of her fugue. "But that means he really did ..."

Again O'Reilly interrupted. "I don't know what that means other than we have a confirmed bomb."

Pollen said, "Jim, we don't have time for this." His tone portrayed the urgency of the situation.

"But if the doctor finds you here, I could get in trouble."

"Just remember, you're the one who brought me into this," O'Reilly said.

She swayed in indecision.

In a soft voice O'Relly said, "Maybe you shouldn't be here."

Mac reached a weak hand out and gave Beverly a reassuring squeeze. "I started this. I have to see it through. This is important. I'll be fine. Go."

Her mouth suddenly dry, Bev swallowed hard and nodded. At the door she said, "I'll be back in three minutes." Then she pulled the door open and walked out.

Pollen blew out a long breath and said, "Tell us how to defuse the bomb."

"I can't. I didn't have anything to do with it. But I do know who can help you."

Pollen shook his head. "If you think you're getting away with this you're wrong. This is terrorism and I can hold you for as long as I want until I get what I want."

"Do you want to stop the bomb, or should I call a lawyer, which will waste so much time the bomb will explode? It's your choice."

Pollen stared hard at him.

O'Reilly stepped in and said, "Look, I believe something very strange happened here. Wherever your information came from, it was right on. Now we need your help disarming it. Can you do that? Are you still able to make contact with the other side?"

"No, that channel is gone. I was in between worlds then. I'm all on earth now. But I can help you."

"Go ahead. Any help you give will be appreciated."

"When Chance Swift heard the terrorists discussing their plot in a restaurant, he picked the pocket of the one who had a flash drive. Instead of going straight to the police with the information, he went home to verify the contents of the flash drive. It was a decision that would cost him his life.

"He believed the information was real, but before he took it to the police, he copied the drive's contents to his computer. Unfortunately, the terrorists had a policeman working for them and he found where Chance lived. They jumped him in an alley while on his way to the police station. Chance beat his attackers and was about to escape when this detective, Hipsher, shot him in the head.

"So what you're saying is the code for disarming the bomb is on Chance's computer?"

Mac looked at Pollen. "And since I've been in a coma, how would I know any of this? I was here when Chance was killed. Have some faith, Detective."

"Well that'd be a lot easier to do if there was a computer at Swift's place. When we searched his apartment there was no computer."

This seemed to puzzle Mac. He scrunched up his face. I was perplexed as well. How had he known about my copying the flash drive on my computer? How did he know I had an apartment? And where was my computer?

Had Dom gotten in and taken it to prevent its contents from falling into police hands? I could understand that. He would be afraid my records might incriminate him, but I never mentioned him. I would never do anything to hurt him. After all, he was my only friend. But if he did take the computer, then it was in the hands of the bomb squad to prevent the explosion. There would be no one coming to the rescue. I had come so far only to fail in the end. My only consolation was that even if it did explode, there shouldn't be any loss of life.

I had heard enough. There was a more pressing matter to

attend to. I wanted to go to Monica. Knowing what pain she would soon endure, I couldn't let her face it alone. I didn't want to witness her ordeal again, but I needed to be with her. As I was leaving I heard Mac say, "Oh, there might be one thing..."

I gave it no further thought. He had given out all the information he could. It was up to the detectives now.

CHAPTER

Sixty-Eight

Joe entered the police station and stood nervously. It had been a long time since he had been in a police station and that hadn't turned out so well. Even though he was clean now and had nothing to fear, old feelings were hard for Joe to overcome. He swallowed hard and approached the desk.

The cop behind the desk had been watching him suspiciously. "Can I help you, sir?"

"Ah, yeah, I guess." He fished the flash drive from his pocket and extended his hand toward the large cop. I'm supposed to drop this off for the detective investigating the murder of Chance Swift."

The cop narrowed his eyes and focused them hard at Joe. "What is this?"

"I don't know. I was just paid to bring it here. So, here."

The sergeant reached for the memory stick, but hesitated. "Let me call the detective handling that case down. You can give it to him personally."

Joe gulped again. This wasn't going like he had hoped. "No sir, I just want to deliver this and go." He dropped the drive on the desk, turned, and started for the door.

"Hey, wait a minute. Who told you to bring this here?"

"It's from Chance Swift."

"It's from the dead guy?"

"Yeah and I was told to say there isn't much time." Joe reached the door and pulled it open, but before exiting, he turned and added, "It's about a bomb." With that, he bolted from the station.

* * *

Monica was still working. I couldn't watch her. I flew back to the standoff. In the short time I'd been away a lot had changed. The cops had dropped back and SWAT had taken up strategic positions.

At the bomb site, a small group of men worked in a controlled intensity trying to learn enough about the bomb to know how to diffuse it. The timer clicked steadily downward. An hour and twenty minutes remained. The bomb squad commander said, "At ten minutes we clear, understood. I don't want anyone close to this thing if it goes."

No one responded.

The grounds were empty of all other people. The police had done a great job of evacuating the site. A perimeter had been established at a half mile radius. Fire trucks stood at a ready to rush in if called. The tension from those working on the bomb extended to those at the perimeter.

Floating toward the food wagon, I decided to drop in and see what was going on. Four people—three women and one man—sat on the floor, their backs to the walls. The two terrorists sat in the middle, their wild-eyed frenzy brought on by fear and the knowledge they had no way out of their situation.

Just to see if I could have any effect at all, I slid into the taller one. I felt him tense. He began looking around.

"What is it?"

"I do not know. It's a feeling; a bad feeling."

I slid into his partner. He shivered. "I feel it too."

The first man stood to peer out the window. His head snapped back and a fine red mist sprayed the interior of the food cart. His body fell backward onto his partner.

The surviving man screamed from shock and pushed the body off. His hands and clothes were now covered in blood. He stared at them and stood, wiping his hands on his pants. A second later, he joined his friend on the floor. There would be no interrogations.

CHAPTER

Sixty-Nine

With nothing else to occupy my thoughts I was drawn toward the diner, not wanting to go, but unable to stop. It was like a 'dead man walking' journey. I feared the end result, knowing I no longer had an avenue to alter Monica's future. The vision I had of her life sickened me.

I sat at our booth and watched Monica move around the diner. Strange how much I loved this woman, especially since I'd never met her. I fought back the tears as I drifted through memories that never happened. She would have changed my entire life, giving me a purpose that had been lost ever since the ambush more than fifteen years ago.

The clock ticked not slowly enough toward quitting time. When her shift ended I stood in the doorway and tried to block her from going outside. I pleaded with her to turn around. I entered her as I did with the sound tech, but she gave no notice.

Less than an hour and twenty minutes were left before the bomb exploded, but less than five minutes before Monica's life as she knew it was over.

As she approached the alley I had to stop. I couldn't go through with it. I wasn't strong enough to watch her total destruction over again. My support was only in spirit. After all I'd seen in my life, after all that I'd done to save other people, I was unable to save the woman I loved.

It happened as before. In a heartbeat they were on her. I dropped to my knees and died again. She screamed and kicked and fought, but the end was the same. They overwhelmed her and carried her into the alley. They swarmed over her.

Then the alley flooded with heavenly light. Shocked from my anguish I looked up. I could only watch, confusion fueling an additional adrenaline rush. My heart warmed with the sight. Had He stepped in with divine intervention? But the light was not coming from above. The sound of people running and shouted demands broke my upward gaze.

"Police! Don't you move."

I tried to comprehend. This wasn't how this went. This was the reality thread. "I don't understand," I said to no one. Was this my miracle? I prayed that it was—that in my dismay I hadn't stumbled into the wrong thread by mistake. Uniformed policemen filled the alley, followed by two familiar men in suits. Pollen and O'Reilly approached the three would-be rapists, now surrounded and cuffed.

"*How*?" Tears of joy washed my face.

"Which one is it?" Pollen asked.

"He said it was the tall one with the missing tooth," O'Reilly said. He pointed toward Toothless and said to a patrolman, "Bring that one." I rushed at him, blew in his ear and watched him shudder. "Ha, take that you bastard."

Two policemen guided the tall man from the alley. They deposited him in the back of cruiser and raced off. Mouth hanging open wide enough to drive a semi through, I turned my attention to Monica, now wrapped in a blanket, being led to an unmarked car. O'Reilly had a protective arm around her. "Monica, I'm Detective O'Reilly. This is Detective Pollen. Are you all right?"

Crying, all Monica could do was nod."

"Don't worry. It's over. They won't ever harm you or

anyone else again. We're going to escort you to the hospital to be checked out then we have someone for you to meet."

He placed her in the back seat.

Recovering enough to speak, Monica said, "I don't understand. Who am I meeting?"

O'Reilly smiled. "A truly remarkable man. Don't worry. He'll explain it all to you." he closed the door and they drove off.

In an instant my eyes filled with tears and my heart swelled to the point of exploding. I had no idea how, but Garrett MacIntosh had just saved my wife. At that point I didn't really care. Monica was safe. My spirit soared, overwhelmed with joy.

While he drove, Pollen took the lead asking questions about the assault. Monica gave what she knew in between heavy sobs. When he was finished Pollen looked at O'Reilly. The big man understood and took it from there.

"Miss Carson, I have to ask you some questions that may seem strange, but I would appreciate honest answers, as they have to do with another case we are working—one that seems to have a connection with these men."

"I'm not sure I understand, but I will try to answer your questions."

"Great," O'Reilly smiled, trying to ease Monica's concerns. "Do you know a man named Chance Swift?"

Monica thought for a moment then shook her head. "I don't think so. Of course, if he's a customer I might recognize his face, but never knew his name."

O'Reilly showed Monica a picture of me displayed on his phone. She took her time looking at it. She shook her head. "No, I've never seen him before." Yet she shuddered as if she'd seen a ghost. Had there been a brief flash of recognition in those eyes?

"Have you ever been in a situation where you were so desperate for help you might have reached out to someone other than the police?"

Monica frowned. "No. What's this about?" She wiped her face with a torn sleeve of her uniform. "I don't understand. How did you know what was going on? Were you watching them? Were you watching me? Don't get me wrong, I'm glad you were there, but …"

O'Reilly smiled. Well, someone was watching. We'll explain all that later. Right now we're trying to see if there's a connection between you and this man. We're trying to determine what this man's involvement might have been with one of your assailants and a bomb that was discovered earlier today. At this point it's unclear if he's a part of it, or a very unusual hero."

Monica gave a quick smile. "I hope he isn't involved. He has nice eyes."

CHAPTER

Seventy

After being checked out at the hospital, Monica was led up to Mac's room. Obvious confusion had her face drawn tight, her eye brows pinched. Caroline smiled at her as she entered. She embraced her and said, “I'm so glad you're all right. I'm Caroline.”

Mrs. MacIntosh gave Monica's arm a squeeze. “I'm Garrett's mother. It's nice to meet you.”

Monica gave a quick unsure smile, but did not speak, trying to comprehend why she was there and who these people were.

“Okay, ladies, let me speak to Monica for a while,” Mac said.

Caroline smiled, gave him a quick kiss, then stepped past O'Reilly who stood in the door. Mrs. Mac followed with Nurse Bev right behind. Bev stopped at the door rose on tiptoe and pecked O'Reilly on the cheek. Then she pushed him out and closed the door, before returning to the far side of the bed. She sat, folded her hands in her lap and beamed as bright a smile as I'd ever seen.

I floated in my usual corner just as curious as Monica to hear the explanation Mac was about to give.

Mac held out a hand to Monica. “Hi Monica, my name is Garrett.” Unsure, Monica touched his hand gently. “It's nice to meet you, although I feel like we've been friends for a long time.” He smiled. “I have a very strange story to tell you about a very special mutual friend.”

Bev's mind wandered as Mac relayed the unusual, but as far as she was concerned, true story of the crossover contact with Chance Swift. Her eyes welled as she came to understand, not so much the magnitude of the event, as much as the heart-lifting beauty of the romance, and the immense power of the love: so strong it transcended death.

Mac began by explaining the circumstances that put him in the hospital. Then he said, “That's when I met Chance Swift, the man who would’ve been your husband.”

It got weirder from there. Trust me.

CHAPTER

Seventy-One

In the days that followed, much media attention descended on the attempted bombing. When Detective Pollen took the podium at the press conference, he gave a play by play account of how his great detective work had tracked down a terrorist cell and disarmed a monster bomb. It was a little over the top, but I couldn't blame him for taking the credit. He sure wasn't going to share it with a ghost.

O'Reilly, however, wasn't afraid to dole out the accolades. "There are two other people who deserve credit for the capture of the terrorist bomber and disarming of the bomb. Garrett MacIntosh, who was responsible for getting the initial tip to the police, and Chance Swift, who gave his life trying to get that information to the authorities. They are both ordinary citizens who became heroes to save the people of this city."

I couldn't deny a slight tingle of pride by being publicly called a hero. It was like getting closure on a life spent trying to do the right thing. Of course, no mention was made of the more supernatural aspect of the case. I mean, who would've believed them?

I had finally become a hero. Too bad it cost me my life. Oh well; the price of fame, right?

* * *

Les was sitting on one of my new recliners. My cloud had taken on a new appearance to say the least. I had pictures of Mac, Mickey and Monica on my invisible walls and tons of sport pictures as well.

I just finished telling him about my miracle.

"So when it was all over I had to go back and follow the thread because I had no idea how they got the disarming codes from my computer. After Joe dropped off the flash drive, the desk sergeant called Pollen, who then called the bomb squad commander. The bomb was disarmed with a half hour to spare."

We were silent for quite a while. I was still excited that things had worked out. My spirit felt much more at rest now. Now it was time to relax and get to know my new surroundings in a much less stressful way.

"I still don't understand how Mac knew about what would happen to Monica, though. You wouldn't happen to know anything about that, would you?"

"Me? How would I know?"

"You know, maybe some inside information from the Big Guy upstairs."

"Sorry to disappoint you, but by the time I submitted your request you had already saved the day."

"Yeah, I did, didn't I? Still, I'm gonna believe I was the recipient of a miracle." I shrugged. "No matter though. Everybody had a happy ending except me, of course. I'm still dead. And I did prove that anything was possible. So ha! Proved you wrong."

Les smiled. "Yes, you most certainly did." For some reason Les was very reserved.

"So what's up? Why so sad?"

"You've become so perceptive. Must have been that

good guidance I gave you."

"Yeah, must have been. You did good, Les. I'm sorry I was so difficult to deal with. Thanks for all the advice and the support."

"And now I must leave you."

I sat up fast. "What?"

"It appears I did too good of a job. I'm moving on."

"Oh, Les! That's awesome. Man, I'm so happy for you."

Les just stared ahead.

"Why don't you look happy?"

His lip quivered. "I'm afraid, Chance. What if Janae doesn't want to see me?"

"Hey, stop. Les, you have spent Twenty-seven years atoning for your lapse. Did you ever cheat on her?"

"No. Never." He shook his head as the tears fell.

"You ever hit her or threaten her?"

"No, I loved her. I would never do that. She was everything to me."

"Do you really think she stopped loving you? She knows all about you. She knows you've paid for whatever mistakes you've made. I'll bet she's waiting for you right now."

"What if she's not?"

"Les, this is the world of ultimate forgiveness. Maybe it's time you forgave yourself. I've become a good judge of people over the years and I think you're one of the best I've ever met, living or dead. Go see your wife. You have an eternity to spend together."

He nodded. Standing up, he wiped his eyes. "You're right."

"When do you go?"

A light appeared from above. "Now."

"Oh!" I stepped forward and hugged him. "I'll miss you, Les."

"Thank you, Chance. I have a feeling I shall see you again, my friend." We went through the motions of shaking hands. He looked upward and gasped. "Oh, Chance!" His voice was choked with emotion. "There she is."

I looked up but couldn't see anything. I guess I wasn't ready to see the Big Time.

"She's smiling. She's waving me to come. Oh, God." His body shuddered as he fought back a sob.

"Go to her, Les. Be happy."

A second later the light was gone and so was Les. I was happy for him, but sad for myself. I was alone now in a strange world. I guess it was time to explore.

CHAPTER

Seventy-Two

When I got down to it, finding people I knew was like searching for friends on Facebook, only easier. I didn't have to follow any of their stupid rules and didn't have to put up with ads, game requests and like requests.

The first group of friends I made contact with was my old platoon mates. We were all there except for one, Theodore Robinson, who was in a Veteran's hospital battling cancer. He was the last of us survivors. We took turns filling each other in on our lives and deaths, unhurried by time or the need to be anywhere else.

It was good to see them all again. I found it interesting that none of us had moved on yet. It was as if we had all been waiting for the entire group to be together again. The bond was still strong after all these years. I felt complete again.

When it was my turn, I filled them in on the whole story and my discovery about contacting the other side. It seemed strange saying that from this side.

"The only bad part was that my killer got away. I wish there was a way to get the bastard."

"Hell yeah, he's a damn traitor," Manuel said.

James added, "He deserves to die."

"No way he should be allowed to live and enjoy life. Not after what he did to you," Eddie said.

Eduardo was the brains of the platoon and he was thinking now. We all watched him expectantly, just as we had done years ago.

He smiled. We knew he had a plan then. “Oh yeah, I got an idea.”

Three days later, I watched as a nurse entered a room occupied by four former military patients. When she got to the fourth bed she stopped and gasped, dropping the chart she carried. Lying on the empty bed, I smiled as she looked underneath then checked the bathroom, all the while a panicked expression displayed on her face. Shocked by the reality of the situation, she ran for the desk to alert security that the comatose cancer patient in bed four was gone.

Quickly, I caught up to my platoon. I knew where they’d be since I supplied the destination. I was only away from them now because I thought it would be fun to see the nurse’s expression when she realized she literally, lost a patient.

Finding the expensive upstate resort had been no problem. I just went back and followed the thread. That was where I found my comrades now. We all hovered outside a small villa set up in the mountains, overlooking the resort and the pool.

An excited buzz ran through our little group. This was better than popcorn at the movies.

“Look, look, look, look,” Russell said, pointing at a cab pulling up in front of the resort’s main building. A large, sickly-looking black man climbed out carrying a small black gym bag. He looked around to get his bearings then began heading up the inclined walkway toward the villa.

He stopped less than halfway there and grabbed onto the railing for support. Hard coughs racked his body. When he pulled his hand away from his mouth it was coated with a bloody spray. The sight sobered us. Robinson was near death. We shouted encouragement.

When we met inside his mind, it had been an easy process to talk him into the plan. He was dying anyway. If he could go out doing something important it would make him feel better about his impending death. We partied for a long while. One benefit of being dead was no hangover. When it was time to go, he wrapped me in a bear hug and said, "This is for you, brother, for trying to save us all."

Now using up the last of whatever energy he had left, Robinson walked up the path toward his target, pulling hand over hand along the railing.

"He's not gonna make it," said Private Smith.

"Yes he will," I said.

We all watched with a mixture of adrenaline rush and sadness, watching the struggles of this once powerful soldier. I felt my eyes well up and my chest expand with pride. I yelled to him, "You can do it, Roby!" The others began chanting his name. "Robinson. Robinson."

At the top of the slope he stopped to catch his breath. He clutched at his chest and prayed. "Please God, just a few more steps."

He straightened his body and gathered his strength. The villa he wanted was thirty yards ahead. As he staggered up the path, Robinson snaked a hand inside the bag. When he got to within ten yards of the villa he pulled the gun out, tossing the bag away.

At five yards, the villa door opened and Hipsher came out looking down at the keys in his hands. He turned to the door and locked it without noticing Robinson closing in. When he turned back, it was to look down the barrel of a .45.

"This is for Chance," Robinson announced, and put a bullet through Hipsher's eye. His body smacked into the door and slid to the ground. Robinson looked skyward as if searching for us. He smiled and gave a thumbs up. Then he went and sat down on a large rock and waited for death, or the police, whichever came first.

My saga was over. With Hipsher's death, everything was complete. My life ended better than I could ever have expected. I was happy and content for the first time since I could remember. Whether I had divine help or not, I would never know, but I chose to believe so.

CHAPTER

Seventy-Three

Afterlife got good very fast for me. Although I tried to keep tabs on those among the living I was still attached to, for the most part, I accepted my new existence and began to enjoy it.

I found an endless baseball game and played with some of the greats. The players would rotate in and jump from game to game, but the innings continued regardless of the score. I was having the time of my death.

I met with the guys from my platoon once a week just to hang out. Robinson joined us long before he could go to trial for murder. It was good to see him. The party we threw him went on for a month.

As for things on earth, Pollen merely scratched his head when he heard Hipsher had been killed. Although it wasn't so much his death that left Pollen wondering, it was learning that his killer was a member of my old platoon. O'Reilly kept at him, but though he waffled a little, Pollen refused to fully acknowledge the existence of ghosts.

Bev and O'Reilly were married a year later. I attended. Bev held a séance and actually invited me. O'Reilly laughed when he found out about the spiritual invitation but he kept looking over his shoulder during the reception. I think he was afraid I was gonna crash it, literally.

Mac and Caroline did get married. I was invited to that one too. Mac talked to me a lot in those first few years. After that, I decided to leave him alone to enjoy his life. Since he couldn't hear me anymore, what was the point? I would see him again someday.

As for Monica, something changed inside her that night. When Mac explained about me, I was shocked to see she wasn't the least bit surprised or disbelieving. Monica said she had dreamed about me the previous two nights. I was floored.

After she left Mac that night, I reached out to touch her; just once. I couldn't help myself. As she stood in front of the bathroom mirror brushing her hair, I entered her body. She stiffened in an instant and gazed at the mirror as if she could see me in the reflection.

"It's you, isn't it?" she asked. She spun fast and wrapped her arms around invisible me. She squeezed me and kissed me. My return efforts were lacking, of course. "Thank you for saving me. I will always think about you."

I stopped in from time to time to see how she was doing, but I had to break from her or my fixation would have been self-destructive.

Eventually, Monica did meet a guy who she cared about a lot, but she refused to marry him. When he gave up and left her, he was unaware that she was pregnant. She moved away, never telling him he would be a father.

She named the boy Chance and that was the last time I looked in on her.

CHAPTER

Seventy-Four

Over time, the members of my platoon began to disappear. Whenever we got together, our numbers seemed to dwindle. There was never any word from our missing comrades. We could only speculate that they moved on to their permanent homes. I hoped I would see them again at some point, but if I didn't, they would always be a fond memory.

I continued playing baseball and looking up old friends, although many friends and relatives I could not find. Perhaps they had moved on already. I might never know, depending on where I ended up. Sometimes I would sit and think back on some people I had known over the years and reach out to them. Sometimes I connected; sometimes not. I didn't dwell on it. But when I did make contact, that first meeting was always interesting. You couldn't make up stories anymore because they always knew the truth. If you had pissed them off or lied to them at some point in your life, they now knew. It made meetings a little awkward, especially when you were reminiscing and said, "Hey, remember when …" and they would answer, "Oh yeah, I remember." Yeah, that got weird sometimes.

Time passed without me noticing. Everything was just what it was and that was fine by me. I gave no thought to my future or ever making a move anywhere. I mean, what more could I want? Then one day, a man dressed in a heavenly white suit that seemed to glow showed up on my cloud. He announced that my time was coming and I should be prepared.

"You mean a decision's been made as to where I am going to spend eternity?"

"No, it's your time to earn your keep. You're to be a transition guide."

"Seriously?" was all I could say. Then he was gone. I thought about Les. I hadn't thought of him in a while. I only hoped I could do as well as he did. I also hoped I wouldn't get someone to guide who was as difficult as I was.

I had no idea when I was supposed to start or where I would find my first victim. I guess I'd know when they wanted me to. I just hoped I wouldn't screw them up too bad.

I was in the umpteenth inning of a game and had just slid in safely to second base with a double when a light caught my eye. As I focused on it, the light morphed into a shape. Then the shape became clearer and a smile stretched across my face.

I called timeout, asked for a pinch-runner, and flew off to the cloud the light had appeared on. When I landed, the man had his back to me. He was scratching his head and studying his surroundings.

"Hi, Mac," I said.

He spun around surprised. Then a big smile crossed his face. We raced forward and went through the motions of shaking hands and hugging.

"Man, it's good to see—oh, damn!—I'm dead then, huh?"

"Yeah Mac, I'm sorry, man."

"Where am I?"

"Ah, this is kind of an afterlife holding tank. It's where

you come when they haven't decided what to do with you yet"

"Oh." I smiled at his confusion. I remembered being where he was now.

"Don't worry, Mac. I'll show you around." Then it hit me. "In fact, I'm your transition guide."

"So, what am I? A ghost, an angel, or what?"

"Well, you look like a ghost, but that's what our life experiences created. Your memories form the pictures that you remember during your life. You're actually just a soul. I'm here to guide you to your final destination."

"So, does that make you my soul mate?"

Now I understood why Les didn't laugh.

I put an arm around him and guided him toward the baseball field.

"Hey, you like baseball?"

"Ah, not really."

Oh well, everything can't be perfect. All in all though, I was about as happy as a dead guy could be.

Other Titles

Random Survival Series

Random Survival

The Long Search for Home

The Endless Struggle

The Journey to Normal

Danny Roth Series

Teammates

Teamwork

Home Team

Stealing Home

Group Therapy

Double Play

Stand Alone Titles

Warriors of the Court

Ghost of a Chance

Live to Die Again

(2019) Mischief Magic

Short Stories

The Con

Short Stop: A Danny Roth short

Super Me

Pick-A-Path Series

Pick-A-Path: Apocalypse 1

Pick-A-Path: Apocalypse 2 (2019)

Pick-A-Path: Apocalypse 3

The Dead Series

Tower of the Dead

Island of the Dead

Escaping the Dead

Made in the USA
Middletown, DE
14 May 2022